More Praise for *And I Do Not Forgive You*

"Every story pulls off a convincing blend of the ordinary and the surreal, and altogether they offer an eye-popping range. One piece will tumble along full of event, and the next will stretch the mind, bit by bit. A single page may erupt in a cornucopia of feeling: groans of heartache, yips of delight, a fine wisecrack or two and the rage of a woman wronged. As a reader, I was so won over I pressed the book on strangers on public transportation."
—John Domini, *Washington Post*

"What joyful play and heart and movement in these stories, full of permission and the thrum of ideas bursting and growing on the page. To read one is like a bon-bon on a silver platter with a lit sparkler stuck inside."
—Aimee Bender, author of *The Color Master*

"Each story feels like it belongs here, but also like it stands alone so well you want to read it on repeat, and while the range of emotions evoked in the collection as a whole is broad, I found myself most often sitting with that indescribable ache that characterizes the bittersweet. . . . With writers like [Amber] Sparks around, the present, at least, is a little nicer than it was." —Ilana Masad, NPR

"Re-appropriating fairy tales, urban legends, and supernatural fantasies, Amber Sparks's startling kaleidoscopic visions recast familiar heroines in their own stories. Reading this was a delight!" —Ling Ma, author of *Severance*

"As this collection points out again and again, we don't live in a reasonable society, but Sparks is doing her best to make sure at least some of the women of our history have their revenge." —Leah Schnelbach, Tor.com

"These stories are fiercely funny, heartrending, enraged and enraging, redemptive—in short, essential. They're also some of the most inventive stories I've read. I loved every one."

—Clare Beams, author of *We Show What We Have Learned*

"With sharp, lyrical wit, Sparks lays bare the inherited violence and misogyny our culture levels at female bodies. While magic ebbs and flows—sometimes working in tandem with technology—no power seems strong enough to put the families and lovers back in their proper place anymore." —Nancy Hightower, *Brooklyn Rail*

"The characters in this third collection of short fiction from Sparks exemplify the famous quote from Muriel Rukeyser that made the social media rounds in the wake of the #MeToo movement: 'What would happen if one woman told the truth about her life? / The world would split open.' These are stories of that split-open world. . . . A collection with a goth heart beating beneath a cheerleader's peppy exterior." —*Kirkus Reviews*

"Sparks' imagination seems limitless, her approaches to style and form without boundaries. . . . At once timely, wickedly funny, and uncomfortably real, Sparks' singular stories have the power to shake us wide awake and shatter every last happily-ever-after illusion." —*Booklist*

"In this genre-bending new collection, Amber Sparks has once again shown herself to be fearless and cutting, the insistent voice that breaks through the hand trying to silence it. I had a lot of fun reading these fresh, sharp, delicious stories, even as my neck prickled with doom."

—Lindsay Hunter, author of *Eat Only When You're Hungry*

"Sparks impresses with her exceptional collection of wry, feminist stories. . . . Some stories smuggle incredible emotional impact into surprisingly few pages. . . . Sparks's sardonic wit never distracts from her polished dismantling of everyday and extraordinary abuses. Readers will love this remarkable, deliciously caustic collection."

—*Publishers Weekly*, starred review

"Irreverent and clever characters take center stage in Sparks's latest collection. The pieces here are beyond the classification of any one genre, borrowing from fairy tales, fantasy, coming-of-age, modern life, and social commentary. . . . Each story is vivid, unexpected, and satisfyingly weird."

—*Library Journal*

And
I Do Not
Forgive
You

STORIES AND
OTHER REVENGES

Amber Sparks

LIVERIGHT PUBLISHING CORPORATION
A DIVISION OF W. W. NORTON & COMPANY
INDEPENDENT PUBLISHERS SINCE 1923

Copyright © 2020 by Amber Sparks

Some of the stories in this book originally appeared in *matchbook, Gamut, Outlook Springs, Wigleaf, The Collagist, Split Lip, SmokeLong Quarterly, Corium, Thumbnail Magazine, People Holding, Grist: A Journal for Writers,* and *PANK.* "A Place for Hiding Precious Things" first appeared in *Fairy Tale Review,* The Pink Issue, edited by Kate Bernheimer (Detroit, MI: Wayne State University Press, 2019).

For information about permission to reproduce selections from this book, write to Permissions, Liveright Publishing Corporation, a division of W. W. Norton & Company, Inc., 500 Fifth Avenue, New York, NY 10110

For information about special discounts for bulk purchases, please contact W. W. Norton Special Sales at specialsales@wwnorton.com or 800-233-4830

Manufacturing by LSC Communications, Harrisonburg
Book design by Fearn Cutler de Vicq
Production manager: Beth Steidle

Library of Congress Cataloging-in-Publication Data

Names: Sparks, Amber, author.
Title: And I do not forgive you : stories and other revenges /
Amber Sparks.
Description: First Edition. | New York, NY : Liveright Publishing
Corporation, [2020]
Identifiers: LCCN 2019029639 | ISBN 9781631496202 (hardcover) |
ISBN 9781631496219 (epub)
Classification: LCC PS3619.P3474 A6 2020 | DDC 813/.6—dc23
LC record available at https://lccn.loc.gov/2019029639

ISBN 978-1-63149-868-8 pbk.

Liveright Publishing Corporation, 500 Fifth Avenue, New York, N.Y. 10110
www.wwnorton.com

W. W. Norton & Company Ltd., 15 Carlisle Street, London W1D 3BS

1 2 3 4 5 6 7 8 9 0

This one's for the ladies.

A curse from the depths of womanhood
Is very salt, and bitter, and good.
—Elizabeth Barrett Browning, "A Curse for a Nation"

What I want is to sleep away an epoch,
wake up as a girl with another kind of heart.
—Lucie Brock-Broido, "Evolution"

Contents

———————➤

Mildly Unhappy, with Moments of Joy   1

You Won't Believe What Really Happened
    to the Sabine Women   7

A Place for Hiding Precious Things   11

Everyone's a Winner in Meadow Park   27

A Short and Slightly Speculative History of
    Lavoisier's Wife   55

We Destroy the Moon   61

In Which Athena Designs a Video Game with the
    Express Purpose of Trolling Her Father   79

Is the Future a Nice Place for Girls   83

Our Mutual (Theater) Friend   87

The Dry Cleaner from Des Moines   93

The Eyes of Saint Lucy   99

We Were a Storybook Back Then   123

CONTENTS

Rabbit by Rabbit   125

Through the Looking-Glass   129

The Noises from the Neighbors Upstairs   133

Our Geographic History   139

Death Deserves All Caps   143

A Wholly New and Novel Act, with Monsters   151

When the Husband Grew Wings   155

The Language of the Stars   159

Mildly Joyful, with Moments of
    Extraordinary Unhappiness   169

Tour of the Cities We Have Lost   173

Acknowledgments   177

And
I Do Not
Forgive
You

Mildly Unhappy,
with Moments of Joy

———————◆

I T ENDS WITH A TEXT, FRIEND TO FRIEND: *I'M OUT*. IT DOESN'T
end, because the other is not.

They become best friends in their late twenties, both
new to the city in the same year, the same sodden winter month. They meet cute, staking out the same spot at
the dingy corner coffee shop to plug in a laptop. They both
cling to the tail end of journalism, that ugly, scaly thing
shrieking for clicks and shares. They laugh about devel-
oping a brand; they share each other's sad little pieces
about lifestyle products and uninformed wellness tips.
They publish fiction no one reads, and in between, they
get married to perfectly lovely people and have three
babies between the two of them. One gets divorced, but
it's not terrible; the ex is an involved dad and he still comes
to birthday parties and makes everybody laugh in a nice,
self-deprecating way. The other stays married and stays
home, eventually, to raise the two babies-turned-children.

She is still hustling, though, because this is the city, and everyone is hustling here, whether it's writing blogs about regional pizzas or selling homemade scented soaps to retailers—which is what the still-married friend is doing. She makes the soaps in her tiny half-bath while her wife half-watches the children.

They understand one another, these two, these best friends, because they know everything there is to know. They know each other's weight, and height, and real hair color, and how often they have sex, and which smells they can't stand. The married one knows the reason for the divorced one's divorce, and she is the only other person on earth who does. The divorced one knows the married one wishes she'd only had one child, and she is the only other person on earth who knows this. They are both mildly unhappy, with moments of joy, in the unexceptional way of most people who live in the city, and they see each other as often as they can these days.

And then, the text. The divorced friend, the receiver, immediately calls. No answer.

Alarmed, she calls the wife. The wife is perplexed. "She's right here," she says. "But she won't speak to you." Then the wife hangs up, having clearly been instructed.

She tries to text her friend again, but her texts are now blocked.

She shows up at her friend's apartment, shouts up at the window, tries to persuade the doorman. Can she throw rocks? It's a fourth-floor apartment, so it's doubt-

2

ful. She's never had any upper body strength. And she might be arrested. Can she make a scene? And where? She considers her options, as a friend. Scenes are for lovers. Friends are supposed to move on. Friends can be ghosted. But best friends?

She feels she's missed a beat, a line. A scene has been left accidentally on the cutting room floor.

After a long time with no posts, her friend's social media accounts are all deleted. The scented soaps website comes down.

She sits at the dingy coffee shop day after day. She stares at the brown and green tiles, picks wider holes in the ripped vinyl chairs. She is hoping to catch her friend stopping by the coffee shop, in nostalgia or apology. It would be very like her friend, except, of course, it isn't.

She calls the wife again; no answer, and then, months later, the number is changed. She stops by the apartment, and the doorman is always apologetic, sympathetic, if embarrassed. Eventually, her friend has moved. The doorman is clearly relieved; he is all but washing his hands of her. The white gloves move imperceptibly.

The doorman thinks (he heard from another tenant) that the friend and her wife moved uptown.

During the school holiday concert, her ex tells her (he heard from a co-op cashier) that the friend and her wife moved to a small Midwestern town. He has dyed his gray hair a dark, obvious brown, and his terrible beige pants match the terrible beige chairs, and with sudden tenderness she wishes they were still married.

The butcher tells her (he heard from another customer) that the friend and her wife moved to a suburb of the city. She has not asked the butcher to volunteer this information. She grabs the crisp white paper and heads home to cry over the pork loin wrapped inside.

She calls all their mutual friends. She has been too ashamed before to do this, feeling sure they will blame her for the break, but now, six months on, she is too distraught to care. The mutual friends have not heard from the friend, or the wife, in months. The mutual friends have not seen the children in their children's Montessori school. The mutual friends have not seen the homemade soaps at the usual retailers lately. Her sweaters always smelled like lilac and jasmine and sandalwood after visiting her friend; now they smell of exhaustion, of thin threads. She does not, she realizes, has never known, the family of the friend; she cannot call or email them to ask. She is not a lover, so she cannot track them down with some great passion.

So now the bread crumbs, few as they were, have been eaten. The trail is tundra-cold. Her friend, it seems, has left the city; or at least, she has left the parts of the city she formerly haunted.

The divorced friend drifts for months, a year, watches old movies during nights filled with half-sleep. She hasn't been this dumb, this ghostly, since she was pregnant. She mourns and does not mourn. She wonders but does not search. And then one night, she makes a decision.

She deletes her texts from the friend who is gone. She

deletes her emails. She deletes the photos on Facebook and Instagram. She erases her voicemails. She tells her small daughter that Aunt Friend was imaginary.

Then the coffee shop closes.

In her late thirties, the friend is a little more unhappy than before. But no matter, and no more than most people who live in the city.

You Won't Believe
What Really Happened
to the Sabine Women

---·✦

AFTER THE ATTACK, WE PULLED OURSELVES SHUT LIKE HOSPITAL
curtains. Snap. They out there, we in here, pain dis-
tilled through tiny wires and tubes. Pain concealed and
compressed until someone has great need of it, until it
becomes a gift.

History will tell you we made quick peace with our
rapists, bore them children, married them. History
will tell you how we launched ourselves into the battle
like burning arrows, how we landed between kin and
assaulters. History will tell you we united Rome.

History likes to lie about women.

What really happened was this: when we saw our
men at war, we almost went out like candles. It's easy to
shrink yourself down when anger burns through you,
hot-fierce, like a grass fire. It sucks the oxygen out; it eats
up all but the most essential parts. Heart, lungs, brain,
blood. Everything else diminishes, shadows itself, clears

out disease. To shrink after anger is such a relief. To run toward oblivion a slaking of dark thirst.

And Demeter saw us scrambling in her fields like mice, and took pity on us, for had she not been assaulted by Poseidon, forced despite all her powers to bear his twins? She knew what it is to carry the weight of so much rage. And so she pulled us into her arms, up with the soil and grass, and she scattered us through the skies as stars, shimmering and immortal in the night skies. And for thousands of years, when men looked at the skies—our husbands, our sons, our grandsons, and so on for many generations—they saw us, and were filled with remorse and remembered what it meant to be a woman at the mercy of men. They built us a temple, with statues of ivory and gold, and every seven years the daughters of Rome wove new dresses for us, from the finest cloth on earth.

Now we are forgotten. We've faded in the sky, and no men remember us. They tell our stories the way they never happened, and though the women can sense that something is wrong, the feeling is too vague for resolution. The halo of lights from the city and the haze from the cars keep us almost hidden from human view.

We are growing jaded, sadder. We can only speak in whispers now. But we still remember our power, what our whispers can warn of, if we aim them at the right ears. Our choice is coming to a head: finally unleash our vengeance, or forget we were ever here.

We cannot destroy man alone. We lost the ability to

do that ages ago. We are so much stardust, and only a little earth still anchors us at all. But it is that little bit that keeps us interested, keeps us watching over the women of this world, waiting, hoping for ones who will say our names. They have only to summon us. They have only to say they've needed us so.

We would swoop down like hawks then, our pain finally put to use, propelling us to the foot of the earth. We would eat evil men like mice. We would rebuild the world in our image, in our glory, in our dazzling beauty and brilliance. Then, only then would we do the thing they say we did long ago: rid them of their wars and bring them peace beyond dreaming, beyond the imagining of any living thing.

A Place for
Hiding Precious Things

ONCE UPON A TIME, IN ANOTHER PART OF NOW, THERE WAS
a girl.

She was graceful and talented and pretty—though no
more than she ought to be—and she was lucky enough to
be the daughter of a very minor king, rich but provincial,
with few real responsibilities. She was delighted with life,
and with her own way of living in it. She loved stories, and
music, and most especially, painting. She loved to create
small strange worlds on paper and had set up a gallery in
several rooms of her home for her art: the royal version
of the family refrigerator. And she had a fairy godmother,
because magic in this part of the world was stronger than
it is in ours, and it lived out in the open and fed on the fat
ripe sun and the clotted cream of moonlight.

Her mother, in the way of most fairy-tale mothers: dead.

Her father, in the way of most fairy-tale fathers:
dreadfully flawed.

The girl herself: naïve; or, charmingly innocent, if you prefer. The girl herself, in the way of most humans: unready for unhappiness.

This fairy tale, in the way of most fairy tales: a warning disguised as a wish.

———

WHEN THE KING'S DAUGHTER WAS YOUNG, he cared little for her, for her drawings or her songs or her stories or her good heart, or for anything at all beyond the alliances her marriage could bring him. Indeed, he was almost a stranger to her. But the girl was not sad; since she'd never known any parent's affection, she didn't miss it. She was raised by nursemaids and governesses and loved by her fairy godmother. She had three cats and two dogs and four turtles, six fish and two ponies, and an enormous library full of books and blue velvet drapery. She had royal playmates and a private lake. She had expensive paints and pretty dresses and riding lessons and music lessons and was probably happier than we'd like to admit a motherless child could be.

But one day, her father happened to look out the window, and he saw his only child riding her bicycle back from the village. He saw her long legs, pedaling gracefully. He saw her long arms, balancing a basket of bread and wine between the handlebars. He saw her long neck, so like her mother's, and he decided (because of course) he must marry her at once. We are to assume, maybe, that he was senseless with grief? Perhaps this is true. Or perhaps the father felt himself entitled to all the world's beautiful women, even his blood relations. This too is not uncommon, in fairy tales or otherwise.

In any case, the girl was properly horrified. She cried until her fairy godmother arrived in her sudden way and hugged the girl tight till her breath was flown. (Fairy godmothers aren't all lacewings and dew, as everyone supposes. They are quite substantial, sturdy as stout trees and deep as rich dark earth, and their love is as good for you as vitamins and vegetables.) The girl's godmother told her not to worry, that she must ask her father for the impossible before she agreed to marry him. But what could be impossible for a king? The fairy godmother—magical but not inventive—deferred to the girl and her artistic imagination.

A dress, said the girl.

Hmm, said the fairy godmother.

But not just any dress.

Hmm, said the fairy godmother.

A dress the exact color of blood, said the girl.

Ah, said the fairy godmother, and smiled. That's *very* good.

BECAUSE THIS IS A FAIRY TALE, the dress is made, and made perfectly. The dress is the exact color of blood, is a bright, saturated wound; it is a monstrous heart made of tulle and lace.

So the fairy godmother suggests a second challenge. The girl goes to her father, who is now impatient as well as incestuous, and demands a dress the color of bone. If the father had not already lost his mind, he would surely have expressed concern at such morbid selections. But he is already lost, and so he demands that the sleeping seamstresses awaken at once and begin sewing the bone dress. The girl begins to pack her trunk, her faith in the fairy godmother diminishing just a little.

As SHE'S DREADED, the dress is the color of bone, a dingy yellow-white shot through with streaks of pink. She models it for the king-her-father, and he closes his eyes in pain. I can't think, he says, why you would want such a thing; it's as though you've turned yourself inside out.

She thinks she could say much the same of him, but she doesn't. She curtsies and waits to be dismissed with a wedding date. Then she runs to her rooms to finish packing.

Where will you go? asks her fairy godmother. And how will you get there? With *his* horses? *His* carriages?

I don't know, says the girl. She understands that she has been ill-prepared for life in the wide world, and she regrets that now. But what else can she do? She won't sleep with her own father, no matter how gone he is. It's escape or death. She doesn't mean to sound so tragic, she says, but it's true just the same.

Okay, says the fairy godmother, and she puts her wide arms round the girl. Her shawl smells of cinnamon and sourdough. (Imagine Cary Grant's housekeeper in *To Catch a Thief*—the one who strangled Nazis with her bare hands—and you have something of the idea.) Okay, she says, here is what we'll do. We'll ask him for a dress the color of death. How could he possibly achieve that? Death is so subjective that no matter what he has made, we'll simply disagree with it. Yes?

Yes, says the girl. And she asks for a dress the color of death to wear at her wedding. I may as well be dead, she says to the king, if I have to marry you.

Most suitors would be somewhat or *very* put off by that, but not our father. He simply shrugs, and agrees, and somewhat ominously adds: This is the last such request I will honor.

When the dress is presented, the girl screams and sticks her hands up over her eyes. It is indescribable, but nearest to a deep black pooled with scarlet and vermilion and mustard and loam—it is the color of rot, the color of flesh in the earth, the color of dust to dust. It is the color of the last bit of tallow before the candle is snuffed.

She cannot disagree that this is death; the seamstresses have done such masterful work. She cannot disagree at all. I will be married in this dress, she thinks, and then I will throw myself from the castle turrets. It will be a fitting shroud.

Oh, come, says the fairy godmother, who is lounging on the girl's lace and lilac bed, prosaically eating a leg of lamb. (And who, by the way, decided fairies were dainty? Spenser, perhaps? It takes a sizable constitution to carry all that magic around, after all.) Wasn't your original plan escape? Let's pack that trunk, then, and get moving, she says, mouth half-full. Your father will want to be devouring *you* (and she has the good grace to shudder here) by nightfall.

THE GIRL STUFFS HER TRUNK in a hurry. Pack light, says the godmother. Bring a little gold, your paints, the three dresses, a toothbrush and some extra underwear. And we need to disguise you, since your father will have his men and dogs out looking for you.

Disguise me how?

The fairy crosses her arms and frowns. She is formidable, even deep in thought. When you run from your father, she finally says, come straight to the stables first. I'll be there waiting. Then the fairy gives a sharp slap to the trunk and it vanishes, WHOOM.

My trunk, wails the girl. What about my toothbrush? My paints? My underwear?

Not to worry, her godmother tells her. This will help you travel light, live in studio apartments, take trains and buses and things. When you want your things, you just snap your fingers in the air and say, Trunk, show up! And obviously, wait until you're alone. When you want it to disappear, give it a good whack.

16

When the girl arrives at the stables, her fairy god-mother is standing over a slain donkey, silver knife in hand. Jesus, says the girl.

Had nothing to do with this, says the fairy godmother grimly. Like most fairies, she respects organized religion, but finds it too tame for her purposes. This is old, wild magic, she says, and the girl finds herself wrapped in the donkey's hide, stinking and bloody and covered with flies and fat globs. The girl is horrified. Clean it with your magic or something, she demands.

But the fairy godmother shakes her head. I can't hide you from your father without masking the scent trail, she says. He'll have the bloodhounds out.

They walk to the wood, the girl trying to keep from fainting. She can close her nose to smells, a trick she learned years ago around ladies and gentlemen wearing too much scent, but she can still taste the metallic tang of blood, still feel the flies biting at her face and hands.

This sucks, she says.

The fairy godmother nods, and stops. With her strong arms, she pulls at the front of an enormous black oak tree, pulls and pushes until it swings open cleanly, reveals an inside thick and dark as night air. It's an abditory, explains the godmother. A place for hiding precious things. Ash is, of course, the traditional choice of shut-away women and spirits, but there isn't any ash around here.

You're going to shut me in a tree? I'd rather die! The girl tries to run but the donkey's head falls over her face, oozing and fly-ridden, and she stumbles over a stump and falls. She didn't think she could weep anymore, and here she is weeping again. This is rotten magic, she says. Just let me die like I wanted to.

Oh, buck up, Melodrama, says the fairy, and she pulls the girl to her feet. I'm not shutting you in a tree—what kind of shitty godmother would I be? I'm sending you on a journey, that's all. It's this first part that's hardest. Then step into the tree, step into a new life. I'll warn you, it's harder for me to cross over into that country. Far less magic there—it's all gone underground. I'll do what I can to help.

The girl hesitates. Her fairy godmother wouldn't trick her, would she? Well, anyway, better than having her father forced on her. She supposes she *would* rather live in a tree. One could tell oneself stories, make friends with the woodland creatures. One could be alone.

Oh, says the fairy. One thing you should know. The donkey skin—burn it. But not until you find true love. You'll lose your chance at love forever if you shed your skin too soon.

The girl stares. Though she is hardly a girl now, she corrects herself—the *creature* stares, glimmers of girl visible in shining dark eye, in small sleek foot. She puts that foot out now, bare and bleeding a little. She steps into the black mouth of the oak tree. She wonders what true love will look like.

WHEN SHE FIRST takes life drawing classes, she thinks, for some reason, about that donkey. She draws the lines over the calves, the human hips, the belly—but she is all the while thinking of the chocolate-colored hide, of her godmother's golden hair come down with the knife, the blood splashed over the straw like ketchup. The sadness and the new freedom of that hide.

She is still living with him now, and it will be a few years yet before she leaves him. He is making them chicken salad sandwiches during a break between classes. She is wearing the bone-colored dress, his favorite, with big black boots, thick-soled and tall. She is still in love with him, in this moment, in this part of the story, and so she put her arms around his skinny back and squeezes. They are both laughing in her tiny kitchen, they are making love under the soft heat of the skylight, they are making sandwiches, they are making time, space; they are making room for someone or no one else already.

They are making a bonfire at his parents' cabin and they are burning the donkey skin. It is something she will never regret, despite her godmother's warnings.

THE BUTCHER IS the first person she meets, upon stepping out of the tree. She finds herself in Central Park, though she doesn't know it's Central Park, and the butcher thinks she might be one of the Shakespeare in the Park actors. He's tattooed from neck to toes, and taking a short break from running his hip-and-featured-on-a-cable-travel-show butcher shop. He's a sweet, funny man, handsome and a little older than her father, gentle even with the dead flesh of his animals. Perhaps it's having lived in the donkey skin for a moment, but she feels drawn to him. He likes her to wear the skin when they have sex. (Don't worry; he cleans and tans it first. And don't worry; she asks him to. It hurts, yes, but she wants to try everything in this new world.) He tells her important things about the place she'll call home now.

The stars, he says, are just salt. The grass is fuel for the animals that feed us. The city is our audience, a million hungry bellies and eyes.

And an animal, he says, is always a dragon that will devour you if you don't respect it. He takes her to the country some weekends, teaches her how to hunt with a bow, to kill with a knife. He teaches her to skin, to flay. He teaches her to preserve a hide.

She uses the butcher's beast blood to make new paintings; she paints startling, painful creatures with thousands of tongues and no heads. The butcher doesn't mind—but he lives alone in a room above his shop, and he doesn't have the room to keep her and her paintings there. So she eventually packs up her things, back into her magical trunk—Trunk, show up!—and she agrees as a last favor to deliver a hog to a roast for a recent art school graduate.

You'll meet some people like you, the butcher says.

Kids who paint, the kind of weird shit you love to paint. Your people.

She doesn't tell the butcher that her people are busy ruling over sleepy seaports, busy discussing casino taxes and port tariffs. She doesn't tell him the only art she ever saw there was hung in the hotel lobbies she toured as a princess. It was her job to bless their grand opening with champagne and a serene smile for the photographers. She wore her best watered silk and knew the paintings were no good.

———

THE ART STUDENT WAS the second person she met. He wore a ridiculous hat and she was, of course, wrapped in the eponymous donkey skin, her protection among strangers. He thought she was a performance artist like him. He made corporate logos out of clay, fired them, then smashed them with a hammer while his friends filmed him. You're an idiot, she told him. And I'm escaping my father. He wants to marry me.

Just like Oedipus, he said, and she never bothered to correct him. It grated on her, years later, and she felt sure she should have said something at the beginning. Perhaps they could have stayed together then, if he had only known his Greek tragedy. Maybe then he would have understood her better, understood how suffering steals the aptitude for happiness from you. Maybe he would have been okay with her melancholy then.

He took her to his tiny place and asked if she needed clothes as well as a place to crash. She said no and yes and snapped her fingers in his tiny bathroom. The trunk came crashing down on the sink. What was that, he said, are you okay in there, I mean, what the fuck?

Yeah, she shouted, throwing on the blood-colored dress. She snapped again to dismiss the trunk and walked out nervously, hoping he would let her stay. His place wasn't much bigger than the butcher's. Her fairy godmother was hovering somewhere over the stove, giving her a thumbs-up and looking a bit uncomfortable by the ceiling. She rarely used her wings.

He's got a trust fund, said the fairy godmother. Good catch!

Okay, said the girl. What is that?

What's what, said the boy. Holy shit, said the boy. That dress is incredible. It's exactly the color of blood.

I'm a painter, said the girl. I want to go to art school. Can I stay here? She almost said, Can I take advantage, but she stopped herself in plenty of time. A life at court had adequately prepared her for every form of falsity, if not much else.

You are so goth, said the boy. He was in awe. He was in love. Yes, you can stay.

She told him his hat made it difficult to tell if he was being serious. Maybe I don't want to be taken seriously, he said, and grinned, and just like that she was his, they were they, on the floor, on the couch, on the counter, on the balcony in warm weather and much to the neighbors' annoyance. (Don't judge her too much. He really was very nice, and very handsome, and an artist at that, and she'd only met older men in her father's castle. And he really did have that trust fund.)

Happily ever after, yes? True love, yes? Unlike the butcher, he was young, he was exciting, he was flexible. It had been suspiciously easy, she sometimes thought. Her godmother stopped showing up after she burned the skin, and she had to follow the days on her own just like any other young woman (albeit with a magic trunk). Except after the endless grinning and the explosion and the joy and the music and the all-night painting sessions and the great, great sex—after all that comes the okay sex and the bad sex, the fights and fallout and the nights spent alone or wishing they were alone. And finally comes the rain, and the last night, always tinged with such poignancy that it feels, just a little, like the page after the last page of the tale, the grin and the hat and the door closed on his face and then nothing. A tape played forward then backward past the beginning.

It was a ring in a cake that finally did it.

She was baking a cake for them both, celebrating her first show. They had friends over, crowded into the tiny flat, and she was wearing the dress the color of blood over a pair of black jeans. Everyone was laughing too loudly, and there was music, and she never could get used to the music here, so bold and brutal, and his jacket was in her way on the counter she was clearing. She picked it up and a ring fell out. It was intricate and silver, and inscribed—and not to her. She put her hands down on the cool countertop, felt the warmth of loss flood her fingertips. Something switched off inside her. She calmly put the ring in her mixing bowl. She watched the yellow swirls of batter slowly snare the silver.

She remembers it now, though she can no longer remember his face or even his hat. She remembers the impossible clang of his teeth, biting down on the solid metal. She remembers the yell, the slow recognition, the way he screamed, You could have fucking killed me. She remembers the friend with the green hair and the Ramones tee-shirt, so red-faced she knew it must be her. She remembers the feeling, finally, of that door closing on everyone. The feeling, not bad, of being alone again. She almost wishes for another love affair, sometimes, just to be able to end it. Just to feel that door close once more. Would that be true love? The relief of loneliness, replayed forever and ever?

THE THIRD PERSON SHE MET was herself. Welcome, she said to herself, and she smiled. She put on a little weight, enough to feel comfortable and soft in her own skin. She got a job in a coffee shop and rented a tiny studio in the building next door. She baked a cake for herself every morning, and every night she walked through the nearby park, just her and the ghouls and the owls. She cut off her long dark hair and created paintings that

made the art world shudder. She watched movies on Netflix with her friend the butcher, and she told him she'd
given up on love. I'm done with that for good.

And you so young, he laughed. It won't be forever. Someone will snap you up. But they mustn't, she
thought, and she was so alarmed at the thought that she
couldn't shake it, all through her midnight walk.

The next night, she asked to borrow one of his biggest
knives. And the next night, she and her dresses (and her
underwear and toothbrush and that useless gold) disappeared, though she left behind her unfinished paintings.
And though art museums will occasionally run retro-
spectives, and a publication or blog might speculate on
what happened to that promising young painter, no one
has seen her again.

But on moonless nights, in deep woods miles outside
the city, some souls say they've glimpsed—just briefly—
someone draped in what looked like an animal skin, huge
head and furry ears fallen back over an elegant neck and
throat. The shape always flees before it can be clearly seen.

Other people just possess you, she'd told her friend,
the butcher.

Is that so bad? he'd asked. To be possessed?

It's the worst fate of all, she'd say. The donkey skin,
she thought, was everything else in the world; it was solitude: anonymous, bloody, and happy ever after.

Everyone's a Winner
in Meadow Park

I'LL BET YOU THINK GHOSTS ARE SO FUCKING ROMANTIC. I'LL bet you think they only haunt rich people, or like, Europeans: pale lords and ladies in castles or governesses in old family mansions. I'll bet you'd laugh your head off at the idea of a trailer park ghost.

Don't.

I WASN'T REALLY RUNNING AWAY when I ran away—I was just hiding. The first time I was seven or so, just after Mum died and I came to live with Maggie. I was probably hiding from Cal, who used to come after me with his shoe, which laugh all you want but it was a big black boot and it hurt like a motherfucker. I was convinced that I could make myself invisible, and nobody could see me hiding on the top of the slide in the park playground.

But the ghost saw me. What are you doing, she said, or really sort of *thought* at me. She was a little like a TV on low, hard to hear unless you leaned in and blocked everything else out. I told her about Cal, it just poured out of me, and she sighed hard like she'd known a Cal or two when she was alive.

I got used to the ghost eventually, but she definitely scared the unholy shit out of me when she first showed up. I couldn't see her, but I could sense her, like a shadow over the sun, you know? Or a cold bit of air under the warmer breeze.

I told Maggie about the ghost one time when she asked where I'd been all bloody day, and she said I was nutters and that unless I wanted to get taken away from her, I'd better not talk any more nonsense like that. Maggie's from England, which is why she uses words like "nutters" and "bloody." (Mum cursed a bloody streak, too, but she learned to swear like an American.) She and Mum were best friends in Liverpool, and they both moved to America shortly after I was born. Without my father, obviously. Nobody knows who he is, except my dead mum. She and Maggie meant to end up in L.A., working in the movies. But somehow they ended up here in Meadow Park, after hitchhiking halfway across the country and running out of money. Maggie met Cal, though, and that put paid to that, as Maggie said. Mum told me we were all going to leave— her, me, and Maggie—and we'd make our way to California. But then the semi collided with Mum's car, and that put paid to that.

MY BEST FRIEND JASMINE is a horse girl. Even when we were really little, she used to hang around outside the stables in Eastbrook and just watch the riders train or whatever the hell they do. Her parents bought her a horse when she turned seven, which explains why it's named Fluffy Marshmallow, or Fluffers for short.

I've ridden a few horses before, and it fucking sucks IMHO. They smell. I mean, I love most animals, especially cats, dogs, but horses . . . I don't know. I have no idea what Jasmine sees in them. But she *really* loves horses—like, obsesses over them. She feeds Fluffers sugar cubes and strokes her mane and draws pictures of her during class when we're supposed to be doing geometry proofs.

But it's not as if you choose your friends, any more than you choose your family. With friends, it's all coincidence and timing and who lives nearby. And we live in the boondocks so options are limited. Thus, my best friend is Jasmine McMahon, who has lived within biking distance of my home-sweet-mobile-home in scenic Meadow Park since we met in Mrs. Cooper's kindergarten class. Her family's not what you'd call trailer park trash, like Maggie and Christmas and me; they live in one of those big houses near Lakeville, the ones with all the tall windows. It's a ten-minute bike ride if you go around the north side of the park.

The ghost thinks she's my best friend, and I have to

keep explaining about Jasmine. Jasmine most definitely believes in the ghost, but she also believes in astrology so idk how meaningful that really is. Jasmine keeps trying to get me to do the Ouija board so my ghost will speak to her, but I'm like, Look, bitch, this ghost is boring as shit like some weird pioneer girl so I hardly want to spend my Saturday night conversing with her *and* Jasmine about crop harvests and oxen. It's the twenty-first century and this ghost needs to move on, you know? She's nice but omg she doesn't even remember her own name anymore, she's been dead so long.

I wish you *could* choose your family. I certainly wouldn't have chosen this one. Christmas, maybe, but definitely not Maggie. And I'm pretty damn sure she wouldn't have chosen me, either. Which is not to say that we don't tolerate each other. Maggie's okay, but she and Aunt Mina (who is actually her mother-in-law, but everybody, including Maggie, calls her "Aunt," idk why, these people have issues, okay) are not the world's brainiest. Maggie never finished high school, even, before she and my mum came to the States. She married Cal right away, and they started a motorcycle repair business, which mostly consisted of Cal fixing his friends' bikes for free. He left a couple of years ago, thank fucking god. All he ever did was get drunk and yell and hit things, mostly Maggie but sometimes me. He sucked so much that even now, thinking about him makes my eyes water and shut like I'm going to get punched in the face any second. I always figured if you had a ghost, they'd protect you, and revenge themselves on anyone who did you wrong. But all my ghost girl ever did was hide from Cal. He seemed to upset her, and she'd dematerialize or whatever when he came after me. Like I said, some ghost, huh? Not much good for spooking people.

Maggie used to try to protect me, though, and sometimes I'd lie to Cal for her and say she was out when she was really hiding out back of the trailer. The night he left for good, we threw a big party and got beer and chips and salsa and rented movies from Redbox. We even got some fireworks and the Johnson kids came over to help set them off. We sat there until like four in the morning, watching the black snakes burn and flake off and fly away over the blacktop. Cal called just once after, and Maggie let me talk to him in pig Latin so he was convinced he had the wrong number.

And we've done okay ever since. Maggie gives me a small allowance to do chores and buy groceries, and take care of Christmas sometimes when she's asleep or at the casino. I guess people can get to depend on each other, even if they don't really belong with each other.

———

JASMINE HAS JUST TEXTED me to say that she's over at the stables again, where she does nothing but ride her horse around and stick its nose in a feedbag. So I decided to head to the library and check out a big ratty copy of *Shakespeare's Plays*. I know this book well—I think I'm the only person that ever checks it out. I love the old-book smell, even though it makes me sneeze. Maggie says it probably gives me allergies, but what the hell does she know? Like she's ever even opened a book in her life.

This time when I get the big heavy thing home, I turn to the tragedies (carefully because the pages are cracking and falling out of their binding). More specifically to *Hamlet*. I want to eat up all the lines, all the words, since *Hamlet* really is the most amazing thing ever written by anyone. I feel the same way every single time I read it—like somebody gave me a very tiny, sustained electric shock and I just can't stop my brain from quivering. Anyway, suddenly I feel like a joint, but I don't want Maggie to know. She worries sometimes that she's a bad influence, as if there were any other kind in this town.

So I go over to the corner of me and Christmas's bedroom, dig around under the bed until I find my own stash, and I roll a little fat joint. I can't find my lighter, so I run to the kitchen, light it on the stove, and then run back to my room. Not like I have to worry; Christmas is napping with Maggie, and Maggie is all conked out on painkillers. I take a drag and breathe out slowly, coughing just a little bit, and then I start with one of Ophelia's monologues, the one about the flowers and herbs after she's gone crazy. I like reading about Ophelia when I'm high—it's easy to imagine myself floating in a river, hair coiling around reeds and floating debris.

The ghost pops up, all wavy air and shadow in my way—she's weird and sudden like that. *Whatcha doing,* she thinks at me. This is weed, I tell her. I offer her some, but she wiggles around uncomfortably. *I never read Mister Shakespeare*, she says, and vanishes. The shadow slips off my book. I don't think they had much education, back in prairie times or whenever.

THE NEXT DAY, Jasmine calls. She's broken again, and she wants me to fix her.

This happens more and more often now, though she's been weird and semi-broken since we were little. Once I caught our mailman standing in her kitchen with his hand up her shirt. I never said anything, because his name was Jimmie even though he was middle-aged, and because he seemed a little slow to me. I suppose I probably should have told someone. He quit about three years ago—hopefully not to become a full-time sexual predator.

Anyway, Jasmine's had a lot of problems all her life, you know? So I'm used to it. I sigh and I don't tell Jasmine that I'm tired of fixing things, though it's true. That's all I do anymore, fix stuff—whether it's Mrs. Morris's busted lip from her meth-addicted, piece-of-shit son, or Maggie's backaches, for which she requires me to get her copious amounts of weed—luckily, my friend Mike Ready is a drug dealer, in a very small-time way.

But I don't tell Jasmine any of that stuff. I just sit in her living room listening to her bitch, and then finally I tell her we're going sledding.

Sledding? She's lying on the couch sort of feet up, and she flips her body around to look at me. But there's pretty much no snow, she says.

I put on my uggo coat, and grab her pretty quilted pink one from the peg on the door and throw it at her. It lands on her head and I can't hear what she says until she gets it off. And by then I have already said, I don't care. We'll use garbage bags. I heard that works. And there might be snow out by the mall.

We make her brother drive us there in his new truck, which we have to pay him ten bucks to do because he's an entrepreneur, which means he doesn't do anything for free. He always turns up his shitty metal real loud so we have to practically yell to hear ourselves. We are very careful to only talk about little things like school and homework and movies we like. We laugh like we always do when we pass by the Meadow Park Casino, with the big neon sign in front that flashes, EVERYONE'S A WINNER AT MEADOW PARK!!!! Four exclamation marks, no kidding. And what a fucking lie—if everyone was a winner, would the parking lot be full of the same Winnebagos, day after day, the owners inside dropping their Social Security money into the slots one quarter at a time? Nobody's a winner in Meadow Park. But everybody keeps trying just the same.

Jasmine has a cure for her brain failure, sort of. She has a little pill case, like old people have where the pill slots are labeled with the days of the week. Hers is pink and the contents keep changing, because the doctors can't quite get it right, the dosage or the pills. Sometimes the medicine starts working, pushing and prodding her until she starts to come out of herself. She does other things those days besides smoke and eat chocolate and draw pictures of horses and wear this old pink My Little Pony bathrobe she got when she was younger (I had a matching one). She'll come over and watch movies with me, and draw these amazing, crazy comics about a group of weird misfit superhero chicks. She'll comb her hair and put on makeup and act like things matter, ask me questions and listen to the answers, and do super well in school without even having to study. She's always been the smartest person I know.

But then the medicine will stop. Jasmine doesn't know why. The doctors don't really know why. Lately it seems like she's always halfway waiting for the days when the medicine stops working. Then her hair goes unwashed, and her parents can't get her to go to school. Then she starts to sleep all day and stay up all night long, lots of times with these strange guys, older guys she meets god knows where. She's more of a ghost than my ghost girl, then. And she draws the damn horse pictures, soft penciled strokes tracing the same lines over the same musculature, again and again and again.

———

SOMETIMES I HATE NOT HAVING a history. I mean, I know a little about the English side of my family, but nothing about my dad's side. Maggie thinks he might have been an American, but she's not sure. My mum never told her. It makes me feel off-balance sometimes, the not-knowing.

We had to do reports in American History last year on our ancestors. It was supposed to show that we're a nation of immigrants, because *everybody* comes from somewhere else. Well, except Native Americans, of course. There are a ton of Guatemalan and Somali kids in my school that like, literally *just* came to the States so their parents and older brothers and sisters could work at the meatpacking plant outside of town.

My ghost was around way back in the day, so I sort of cheated and asked her about her own family. Normally her conversation is so absolutely boring, all gardening and sewing patterns, but this time I was taking notes like "Oh what tell me more" so fast I couldn't get it all down.

When it was my turn to give my report, I said that my ancestors were Swedish farmers who bought their land cheap from the railroads when they came to America in the 1800s. I talked about how their farms failed one bad summer, how the crops just sat there unsold and rotting. Ms. Nivens got all teary when I got to the part about how my great-grandfather Sven finally gave up on the farm, sent his sons off to work in the stockyards and his daughter off to be a maid, and hung himself in his own grain elevator.

Sven was really the ghost girl's dad. That's her story. It was easier than admitting I didn't have a story of my own.

It seems like nobody writes really *grand* stories the way they used to. I mean, I've always loved all the stories and novels and poems and plays where it seems like the author just took everything that's ever been true about life and people, and stuffed it into the pages and let it grow out like some strange, bloody, chaotic plant.

I don't think that the things that happen to people nowadays are any less grand and spectacular than they used to be—it's just that nobody writes about the new big stuff anymore. Or at least nobody we read in high school. The stories have gotten so small. All this stuff they want us to read, like, cool, that's great that this kid is hanging out at some grocery store or whatever, okay, but are you going anywhere with this? Because, meanwhile, this kid that used to live in our park, Dan, just a few years older than me, just OD'd and died. Junk cut with worse junk. And this spring some kids just disappeared from my school and we found out they got deported after the government raided the packing plant where their parents worked. And people are getting killed in genocides and terrorist attacks all over the world, and dying of starvation and rioting about food. I mean, it's not like we're lacking for big stuff to write about here.

For me, I just like to see all the people and places and emotions and conflicts and struggles all exploding out of the pages of one single amazing book. Because that's how life really is, right? You don't get to just sit there and concentrate on one tiny little thing. Life just comes at you from everywhere and you have to deal with it all at once. Human life is a huge, messy, complicated, unbelievable thing. No wonder some people still don't get that we used to be apes just flinging our shit at each other.

———

THE GHOST FINDS ME when I come home and sort of drapes herself over me, all warm and sad and invisible. Aunt Mina is in the kitchen, drinking a Diet Coke and gossiping with Maggie. I slide past her to get to the fridge and grab a Coke for myself, and when I open it, I notice she's just staring at me. In this intent, focused, batshit kind of way.

Aunt Mina terrifies me. She's the craziest old lady. I try to run past, but she grabs my arm and holds me there, smoking with her free hand and looking not exactly at me but sort of past me, her eyes a little bit unfocused. She blows smoke out of her nostrils, which makes me cough, and she slowly shakes her head in this way that reminds me of one of the really old-ass sea turtles at the zoo.

There's a dark aura, she says. She coughs a gross wet cough, and I try to get loose. Tragedy envelopes you, child, she says. It *surrounds* you.

I have no idea if she means the ghost or me.

Aunt Mina knows all about tragedy. Everyone says so. She smokes long, thin cigarettes, and wears tons of jewelry, so much that she clanks and creaks and jangles when she moves. She owns her own business, out of her duplex. It's a small room with green curtains and a super old computer and super loud printer and a whole bunch of ashtrays. When she prints stuff, the neighbors bang on the walls and the dust comes up all around you, like a filthy snow globe.

She used to be in love, a long time ago, way before I was born. Not with her husband, which is part of the tragedy. She had an affair, and they had a baby, and the baby was Cal, I guess. Apparently everybody knew, even her husband, but he must not have cared because he stayed married to her for another fifteen years until *he* died of cancer. And then Cal abandoned her too, which good riddance really, so she kind of adopted me and Christmas and Maggie. Anyway, she's a very strange old lady—*really* old, with skin so thin you can see all these purple veins underneath, and brown stains on her hands and cheeks. And now she stares at me with those weird watery eyes that old people have, until I kind of shake myself free and slither around her to the bedroom. The ghost sort of relaxes, like a coil unwinding. I can tell she thought Aunt Mina could see her.

I know I've been bitching about the ghost girl, but I don't want you to get the wrong idea. She's okay. I imagine most ghosts are boring—if you stick around long enough without doing any changing it must make you pretty stale, sure. But I think maybe she's here to protect me or something. Lately she's gotten much bolder. Yesterday, for example, the ghost girl saved me from Mike Ready. We were sitting on a picnic table in the Randall

Park shelter, and he just kind of leaned over and grabbed me with one arm and tried to unzip my jeans with his free hand. He mashed his face into mine, like something would happen if he kept it there. I actually thought for like half a second that he must have lost his balance and fallen into me, before I realized what he was doing. I tried to move away but he was holding me pretty tight. I felt the ghost then, felt the weird sizzling energy that comes off her, and it smelled angry, *burnt*. I felt her push that power forward, like a magnet, and Mike fell back and right off the table. He hit his head on the bench and landed in the dirt. It was kind of funny, but I didn't laugh because I didn't know who else I'd get Maggie's weed from if Mike wouldn't sell it to me.

What the fuck did you push me for, bitch? Mike stood up, pissed, brushing the dirt off his ass.

I shrugged. I dunno. I like somebody else, okay?

Who?

Nobody you know. A senior. I thought this was smart of me. Mike would never want to get in a fight with a senior, so he probably wouldn't ask any more questions.

Huh, Mike kind of grunted at me. Well, don't think I'm gonna sell you any discounted stuff anymore, he said. You can pay the same price as everybody else.

I sighed in relief. So you'll still sell to me?

Business is business, he said. And anyway, you're not that hot.

Mike's dad owns a cherry-red Camaro. He parks it in his driveway in the summer and washes it by hand every weekend, wearing teeny-tiny shorts and no shirt. It explains a lot about Mike.

But I had to tell the ghost girl off. I know you lived in like, violent times, I said, but nowadays you can't just go around pushing people. They'll get pissed and push me back, because they don't believe in you. She seemed upset, and vanished pretty quick after, which is okay because I needed some time to myself, and ghosts are real goddamn needy, you know? Even the good ones.

◆————

OUR SCHOOL JANITOR, Mr. Pete, told me to come downstairs to his office today after PE. (His name is John Pete, two first names, WTF right?) I was freaked out but a janitor's almost like a teacher or principal—you can't exactly say no. His office is next to the boiler room, so it's hot and creepy and dark and there are plenty of places a person could hide if they wanted to ax-murder you or something. When Mr. Sweeney was the janitor, it was even creepier, because he was old and crabby and reeked of alcohol. Even the senior guys kept out of Mr. Sweeney's way.

But I think Mr. Pete is worse. Jasmine disagrees; she thinks he's gorgeous. And he is good-looking, sort of, with slicked-back black hair and big eyes, and he's probably just middle-aged or so, but there's just something gross about him. He gives off bad vibes. I think it's telling that the ghost girl never, ever sticks around when she sees him. She oozes right out of this dimension like

AMBER SPARKS

butter melting. And now I've worked myself up and I get all sweaty again between my nervousness about Mr. Pete and my nervousness about the hiding ax murderers. I run-walk the rest of the way downstairs and practically bang on the office door.

Hello, I mean to say, but instead I think I say Help. Omg. What a total loser I am.

Luckily, Mr. Pete is busy opening the door so I don't think he hears me anyway.

He smiles at me and asks me to sit. Then he reaches into his desk drawer and pulls out a book. I thought you might like to read this, he says, handing it to me. You being a fan of the Bard and all. It's a copy of the Sonnets. This is not what I was expecting, and "the Bard"? God, what an asshole. But it's a thoughtful gesture, and I know you're supposed to be polite to authority figures or whatever, so I smile and take the book.

Thanks, I say, and get up to go. Mr. Pete reaches over the desk and grabs the strap of my bag, sort of playfully yanking me back with it.

Now bring that back in one piece, he says, and when I put my hand on his desk to steady myself, he puts his hand over mine and smiles again, a big white wide smile straight from a toothpaste commercial. I am really nervous now. And not in a good way.

Uh, thanks for the, uh—thanks for the book, and I'll bring it back—thanks—I have to go to class, I say, and sort of back out of the office. I run all the way up the rickety old steps. It's not like Mr. Pete is an ax murderer or anything—but I can picture him hiding in that basement just the same.

Maybe he's just lonely. Maybe he wishes he taught English? Maybe he never knew anybody else who liked Shakespeare. But how did he know I liked Shakespeare? Maybe the librarian told him? But Ms. Lisa just wouldn't, I can't imagine. Maybe Maggie did?

I'm too riled up to go to class, so instead I walk home and sit at the picnic table in the park. Someone has carved a big crude heart into the top of the wooden table. I run my finger over it again, and again, until I get a splinter and I have to go inside and dig Maggie's tweezers out of her top dresser drawer. Luckily, she's all passed out in front of the TV so she doesn't even notice.

It makes me sad when I think of Maggie, and how she probably should have married somebody like Ted Tyler. Ted Tyler owns Tyler Tires, which recently expanded into a regional chain, and he makes a shitload of money. He always whistles when Maggie walks by with Christmas in her stroller.

Maggie used to be pretty. I've seen her old photos, from way back when her hair was like forty feet high. She probably could have been a model back when big hair was a thing. But I think she just wore all the pretty right off. Before she hurt her back, she worked the overnight shift at Cub Foods, stocking shelves. She'd come home, sleep for a few hours, and go to her other job cashiering at Walgreens. She had to work two jobs, because Cal could never even hold down one. He would work construction sometimes, or fix cars for his friends, but he always got fired for stealing or fighting or drinking on the job. The worst was when he got a job parking cars at a used car lot, and he got so drunk he ended up driving a beat-up little Chevy Nova all the way home and parking it in *our* lot instead. Maggie managed to convince them that it was all a misunderstanding, so the car lot agreed not to press charges, but Cal still got charged with drunk driving. And fired, duh.

Anyway, after Christmas was born, just before Cal left, Maggie fell asleep and fell right off the ladder at the grocery store while she was stocking. She can't work anymore, so she gets disability, but it's not very much money for three people. And she has this chronic back pain that makes her cry sometimes. It really sucks. Nothing helps except smoking weed, which is why she's going to kill me when she hears the price is going up.

Sometimes I wish Ted Tyler wasn't married, so he could come and take Maggie (and Christmas) away with him. He would treat her pretty well, I think. You can tell by the way he looks at her. But I don't know what I would do then—maybe go live with Aunt Mina? Clean the ashtrays and listen to awful old-people stories? Anyway, Ted Tyler *is* married. His wife and Jasmine's mom are friends, and they always throw these stupid jewelry things where you think you're going to a party but really you're just there to buy stuff. In fact, they're throwing one tonight, which is why Jasmine is sleeping over at my place.

I hate when Jasmine sleeps over. I have to sleep in the same bed as Christmas, and somebody always picks that night to come home drunk and start yelling and waking up the whole park. And the ghost girl gets nervous when men start yelling, so she wraps around me like an electric blanket and talks a boring blue streak about harvest season when she was alive and Jasmine can't see the ghost girl or hear her so I can't even show her off like you'd think a ghost would be good for.

———

I'M CURIOUS ABOUT the ghost girl, too, in case you're wondering how dull can I be? I know ghosts only come back to haunt the earth when something truly fucked up happens to them, and I'm not so sure I really want to know what happened to my ghost. It's not like I haven't tried. I've Googled murders and suicides and stuff and I mean, part of the problem is that I live in a stupid suburb and I don't know where the ghost is from. She doesn't seem to know either—she can remember all kinds of dull shit about milking cows and old cars without windshields, but she can't remember many things about herself. She says it's all been blurring for a long time.

So today I decide to take what I know and head to the library. Hey, I say to Ms. Lisa, my fave librarian. She's read basically every book in the world and looks like a movie star, but she only dates women. I think that's pretty brilliant, but in a town like this one, that makes men mad. And women too—Jasmine's mother says she has "nothing against gay people" but that Ms. Lisa is "wasting her beauty." I think she just says that because Ms. Lisa has better things to do than come to a Tupperware party.

Hey, says Ms. Lisa. She's wearing a tiara today. I don't ask. I'd date her, though. What do you need? she says.

I need to know about tragedy.

Ms. Lisa looks at me weird. Her eyes are huge, but she narrows them and asks, Fiction about tragedy? Novels? Short stories?

No, like true crime kind of tragedy, I say. Did anything bad ever happen around here to a young girl? Maybe my age or a little younger?

Ms. Lisa comes around the desk and takes my hand. I don't mind. She looks real fucking serious, though. She takes the tiara off. Okay. Like glasses for the modern librarian. Are you scared of somebody? she says. Is there anything you're afraid of, honey? You can tell me.

I don't want to, but I pull my hand away. Naw, I say, but something about the way she asked has me way more scared now than when I came in. I just wondered if there were any ghosts around here, I try. Like for ghost hunters, you know?

Ms. Lisa's eyes narrow even more, until they're practically closed. There are ghosts in every town, she says, and shakes her head. But I wouldn't go hunting for them.

Tonight the Andrewses' dog Snotty, a big huge white dog that's part wolf, gets loose and starts running around the park howling like mad. The two stupid Andrews kids, Tina and Angie, start running around after him, shouting brilliant things like, Here, Snotty! Snotty boy, come back! Snotty, we love you, Snotty!

Over in my bed, Jasmine starts giggling. She's trying to hide it, burying her face in the pillow, but her whole body is shaking and I can tell.

Shh! I tell her. You'll wake up Christmas. That just makes her laugh even harder.

I sigh loudly and turn over in bed. The ghost girl is suffocating me and I seriously wish she'd disappear for one damn night. Jasmine always does this. And tomorrow morning, she'll tell her mom and dad all about the trashy mobile home comedy.

It's not that I want her life. Horses and wall-to-wall carpeting and a perma-tan mother? No thank you. It's just that I don't want my life to be amusing. I don't want my life to be small and funny and disposable.

We could go to your place, I tell Jasmine. We could sneak out and go to your place and watch some horror movies on Netflix. Jasmine hates horror, and she thinks fantasy is stupid. Why would I want to read about things that aren't even real, she always says.

Real life is boring, I always say. Don't you ever want to escape?

Every damn day, she always says back. But when I do, I'll do it for real.

THE NEXT MORNING, Maggie takes me and Jasmine and Christmas out to Denny's for breakfast. The ghost girl doesn't come—she seems to have her own shit to do some days—but it's still a total disaster, as it usually is when Christmas goes anywhere. She spills her Coke all over the table and screams because she has to sit in a booster seat. I don't blame her—it's one of those hard brown plastic ones, and it's got some kind of sticky goo all down one side of it. I order a Grand Slam and eat every single bite, dipping my sausage links in the syrup over and over again until they're nice and saturated. Jasmine glares at me because she says she's watching her weight and I don't have to. I'm straight like a pencil. I wish I had a figure like Jasmine, though I wouldn't want all the attention she gets from the senior guys just because her boobs are huge.

AUNT MINA IS in her office, chain-smoking as usual, "D-I-V-O-R-C-E" playing very softly in the background while she sits there typing. She loves old country music, Aunt Mina. She can't get enough Tammy Wynette and Crystal Gayle.

I have been told to march myself right over to Auntie Mina's and keep her company. I am totally horrified by this direct order from Maggie, and only the slightest bit of pity makes me ride my bike past Jasmine's and on to Aunt Mina's. Especially since Jasmine has just texted me to see if I want to go ice skating, which I do. Damn. *Entertaining crazy old lady*, I text back. *Sorry.*

Mina stops typing for a second, and spins her chair around. She jams a cigarette between her lips and waves her hands at me. Here, what are you doing? Stop playing with your phone and get me my lighter, she says, and I dig it out of her crusty old purse. There are a million balled-up Kleenex in there. So you know, she starts, I have lung cancer.

I just kind of stare at her, not sure if she's kidding. I mean, she must go through three or four packs a day, so I guess I wouldn't be surprised. Maybe it's mean, but I have to ask, For real?

She squints her eyes at me through the smoke around her face, as if I might have turned into someone else there for a second. Yes, for real. I found out a few weeks ago. She takes a deep drag off the cigarette and blows smoke out of her nostrils in this totally dramatic, gross way. She reminds me of a character in a Chekhov play. You know, the ones that always seem to be living about forty years in the past? But she's not Russian. She's from Nebraska, and her family came over from Iceland, if you can believe that. I mean, who moves here from *Iceland*? Are there even *people* there?

Jesus, so why don't you quit smoking, then? I don't mean to say it, but it's out of my mouth before I realize.

She does that squint thing again. She's got some crazy wrinkles, Aunt Mina. When she squints they come out in big dents all over her yellowy face. Oh, right, I'm going to quit now, she says, and laughs. It's already killed me—what else could it do to me? Then she gets this really serious look and turns so she's facing me. She smells like old people: that stuffy, decaying, B.O. smell. I don't want to look at her, so I pick up a little ballerina statue she has sitting on the coffee table. It's one of those stupid statues where the figures are doing adult things, like dancing and getting married and holding babies, but they have little-kid faces with great big eyes. Mina has a whole lot of those.

Put that down, she snaps. That's valuable. I put it down and sigh loudly.

Have you told Maggie yet? I ask.

No, she says, and I don't know that I will.

That makes me mad. I mean, Maggie's no angel, but she's had a fairly shitty life and this is just going to be another shitty blow in it. And I think she deserves to know that her own ex-mother-in-law is dying. So, naturally, I tell Aunt Mina that.

She stubs out her cigarette and puts both her old spotty hands on her knees like she's steadying herself for something. I've never seen so many rings on one set of hands. She does the serious look at me again, and again I have to look away and quick pick up the stupid big-eyed kid statue again, like it was the most interesting thing ever on the planet. Oh, wow. Look at the way somebody

painted the tiny eyelashes on by hand. What a total fucking waste of time.

Oh, honey, she says. She has not ever for real *ever*
called me honey before. I'm leaving everything to you,
she says. The house, my money—all of it. You're the only
one who'll ever amount to anything—maybe you can
use it to go to college, huh?

You know how people in movies are always dropping things when they get surprised? And you're like,
Yeah, right, who does that? I dropped that big-eyed ballerina kid statue so quick the thing shattered into forty
million pieces.

I AM NOT SUPPOSED TO tell anybody. Aunt Mina said so.
Not yet, anyway. I try to be good. But I really do want
to tell Jasmine. I want to tell her that with my money,
she won't have to worry anymore about her horrible
mother or her messed-up brain. We'll have enough
money to leave this town behind and head for L.A. or
New York or someplace, be real people somewhere.
Make good the way my mom and Maggie never did.
Stop getting stuck. Maybe I'll tell Jasmine I love her,
that I always have, you know? Maybe the ghost girl
will come with us, too. Maybe she's as ready to move
on as we are.

Then she's here, the ghost, saying *Hurry hurry*, and
I think damn I guess I'm right, this chick is in as much

of a hurry to leave this place as me. Yeah yeah, I think at her, but her power is a wind, is a huge muscular wind flying me forward, like she's never done before, and I feel scared and small and dangerous all at once. She's pushing me toward Jasmine's, so fast the fields and chain stores blur into one brown smear, kind of apt I think haha but I am suddenly there like some seven-league boots and before I can freak out properly I see the car, Mr. Pete's car, and he's putting something in the trunk. *Hurry hurry*, says the ghost. *It's almost too late.* I rush to the trunk and Mr. Pete freezes, and I look and it's *Jasmine*, tied up and struggling, and her eyes are so scared, holy fucking shit what would you do, and Mr. Pete starts toward me and I think *Oh shit I'm dead, we're dead* but the ghost girl pulls my voice out like yarn into a thick, tight scream, on and on, unwinding until the neighbors start outside. Mr. Pete is stuck still, his trunk up, his legs rooted, and the sirens scream and Jasmine is free, is sobbing, is on the ground saying I didn't mean to, I didn't mean it and her mom is there crying too like I didn't even know that bitch could cry actual tears and everything just seems to go on and on like none of it is ever going to stop. The ghost girl holds my hand, electric fist in mine, and I can hear her thinking *It's okay now*, but of course it isn't. What kind of tragedy is *this*? It's not grand and operatic at all; it's just awful, just like all the other awful hurts that happen to people like us.

This is *not* the kind of surprise where you drop

things, or jump up and down, or faint, or even let your jaw fall like characters in books. This is a different surprise. This is the kind of terrible surprise where you just sort of stand there, doing nothing, holding your hands in fists. This is the kind of surprise where your insides quietly eat each other, and your brain goes dark and red and sad.

A Short and Slightly Speculative History of Lavoisier's Wife

L AVOISIER'S WIFE WAS A CHEMIST; OR RATHER, LAVOISIER'S wife was a *chimiste*: from the Latin *alchimista*; see also "alchemy."

Lavoiser's wife was a *chimiste*, a term first used cattily, contemptuously—a term first linked with palmistry, sophistry, casuistry. The *OED* seems to be telling us, *wink wink nod*, that chemistry once held hands with charlatanism. But! Lavoisier's wife! Was, in fact, a mover and shaker in chemistry's side business of buying respect. *(R-E-S-P-E-C-T, find out what it means to ions and she!)*

Lavoisier's wife was buried in 1836 in Père Lachaise Cemetery, in Paris, alongside her husband. Did You Know: Pere Lachaise was the very first modern cemetery in Europe? Not the kind chained to the church, with the best bodies piled up under the altar—but the smooth green lawn, Elysian Fields-ish kind that a respectably diverse, even irreligious citizenry might be interred in?

Lavoisier's wife was rather modern, in a century where modernity and superstition were two ends of a long, tattered rope bridge.

Lavoisier's wife—not time, not contemporaries—secured his place in history. (As is, must we point out, so often the case?)

Lavoisier's wife, once upon a time, went out to lunch and when she came back her husband and her father had both been eaten by a savage, starving wolf.

Lavoisier's wife was a woman, yes, and a character of courage, yes. And as such, was undaunted by the state-sanctioned murders of her husband and her father, and by the seizure of her husband's papers during the Reign of Terror. And by some other threats made at her and toward her by Friends of Marat.

Lavoisier's wife said, Screw these revolutionary assholes.

Lavoisier's wife held up a glass to show us not everything about the French Revolution, or indeed any revolution, was enlightened.

Lavoisier's wife knew that reactionaries are often, well, reactionary.

So Lavoisier's wife wrote a preface. The preface was to accompany his final work and memoirs, and was basically a middle finger to his contemporaries, whom she blamed for his death.

Lavoisier's wife was like, Do you see me over here writing this preface?

Lavoisier's wife was like, Do you see me over here demanding the return of my husband's papers?

Lavoisier's wife was like, What are you going to do to me? Which was quite brave, because she certainly knew exactly what they could do to her.

Lavoisier's wife had no more fucks to give.

Lavoisier's wife was called Marie-Anne, and in full Marie-Anne Pierrette Lavoisier, née Paulze, but for the purposes of this narrative she shall be known as Lavoisier's wife. This is not intended to strip her of her humanity or personhood, as a woman; rather, it is meant to focus a tight and somewhat ironic spotlight on the role she will play in her husband's drama, and to signal (*wink wink nod*, as the *OED* would do) her eventual and historical erasure from it.

Lavoisier's wife eventually married a second time, a man named Benjamin Thompson. Or if you want to get fancy, call him Count Rumford. But whatever you call him, know that this is not the end of one love story and the beginning of another. (And indeed, life rarely is.)

Lavoisier's wife remained *Lavoisier's wife*, that is to say, she did not change her old married name to match her new husband's. *Interesting*, as polite society said.

Lavoisier's wife apparently really pissed off Count Rumford, what with her refusal to take his name and also her general absolute devotion to her first husband's work.

Lavoisier's wife apparently liked to tell stories—*soooooooooo* many stories, as Rummy would say—about her dead husband and the good times they had together, doing chemistry stuff. Sure, it was probably kind of annoying. But you know, when someone's husband gets decapitated in a revolution, you make allowances for them. But not Mr. Thompson, a.k.a. fancy-pants Count Rumford. Nope. He complained, like an asshole. And this did not go over well.

Lavoisier's wife probably said something like, Oh, Mr. Thompson, didst thou discover phlogistan? Dost thou even know what phlogistan is? Yeah, prithee I did not think so.

Lavoisier's wife probably didn't say exactly those words, but you know, we want to give the sense here that we are waist-deep in the past. At least ankle-deep.

Lavoisier's wife is an important historical personage, and in restoring her reputation, we do not want to give the impression that she was a *contemporary* woman. Understandably, that would be false. Lavoisier's wife was without doubt a helpmeet, or would consider herself so. And though she was herself an accomplished woman, it was her husband she would help make famous.

Lavoisier's wife did not sound like a sitcom character, of course. We are sorry to have previously given that impression. History does not record any extraordinary level of sassiness on her part.

Lavoisier's wife, perhaps, may have sounded more like her rough contemporary, Charlotte Corday. Corday, though a bit younger, was also from a good family, convent-educated.

Perhaps then they could have been friends, had Corday not been, you know, guillotined on the Place de la Révolution. Maybe they could have started a zine, could have conducted their own chemical experiments. Perhaps they could have discussed the practical problems of being broad-minded women when women were basically just broads. Perhaps they could at least have had coffee and croissants and bitched about the nuns.

Lavoisier's wife, though—back to Lavoisier's wife.

Lavoisier's wife was an accomplished woman in her own right, as we implied before.

Lavoisier's wife studied with Jacques-Louis David, the famous painter, the better to draw and sketch her husband's methods and apparatuses.

Lavoisier's wife was a very *accomplished* helpmeet. Nowadays you would refer to her as a *lab assistant*.

Lavoisier's wife, not to brag, but she spoke more languages than Lavoisier, and used to translate whole books into French just so he could read them.

Lavoisier's wife, let us repeat, *translated a shitload of science books into another language* just so her husband, audience of one, could understand what they said.

Lavoisier's wife, in fact, upon further research, was probably more of an equal, a co-collaborator, than a helpmeet. Isn't that the most dreadful word, *helpmeet*? Should we look up the etymology, because that's what one does in these sorts of faux-scholarly pieces? Oh, would you look at this, *helpmeet*: "from the Bible, Genesis 2:18, 20, where Adam's future wife is discussed as 'an help meet for him.'"

Lavoisier's wife surely could have used a barf emoji, had she ever looked up the origin of "helpmeet" and shared it with Charlotte Corday.

Lavoisier's wife's text: *Can you even fucking believe this shit?* (barf emoji here)

Lavoisier's wife's text back from bff Corday: *OMG OF COURSE GENESIS, WTF*

Lavoisier's wife considered herself a scholar, and owned her own large library with hundreds of books. We consider her a scholar, too.

Lavoisier's wife received her formal education in a convent, where she was placed after her mother died.

Lavoisier's wife's mother died when she was young. Just like a character in a fairy tale, her mother disappeared early along the path. Lavoisier's wife was just three.

Lavoisier's wife did not exactly live, though, in a fairy tale. Did we mention she was married off at thirteen?

Lavoisier's wife was a child bride, basically. Talk about making the best of a bad situation. Does this sound too much like a joke? A punch line? We are not joking. Or at least, if we are joking, we are making the sort of joke that's referred to as whistling in the dark. We are crying in the aisle of this drugstore. We are buying lotion and lipstick and thinking about a woman who's never had a name, down all the corridors of history, doomed to smudged margins and funny little footnotes.

Lavoisier's wife had an internal life, even at three, even at thirteen. Do you believe in it?

Lavoisier's wife is buried in Pére Lachaise. Her tombstone says, *Here lie the mortal remains of Madame Marie-Anne Pierrette Paulze Lavoisier, Countess Rumford.*

And what is history, anyway, but the chance to dig up our skeletons and give them new stories?

We Destroy the Moon

"In the dark times will there also be singing?"
"Yes. There will still be singing about the dark times."
—BERTOLT BRECHT

———————————•+•➤

A T THE END OF THE WORLD, YOU DISCOVERED WORDS COULD change. You had always been good with the infrastructure of language; you excelled at making roads and bridges out of speech. I could have forgiven you almost anything in that first crisis, anything but the loss of surety in sentence and letter and sound. The first of the flyers you tacked up around the city read, TIRED OF THIS TROUBLED WORLD? COME DOWN TO THE TEMPLE TONIGHT AND MAKE PREPARATIONS FOR THE NEXT WORLD. But I didn't want the next world. I was more tired of you.

I considered the words we typed and shared, what trended, what was tossed. I swore not to be like you—a scam artist; or like them—the scammed. I took notes and I took screenshots and I researched meanings. I wrote down etymology and comforted myself in language's long and twisting track record, shaped and reshaped, long before we got here.

YOU WERE BORN the year we traded leaders for towers. The Sears Tower went up not long after Johnson died, when the country had to wait half a year just to have a former president. Then the World Trade Center after Nixon resigned. You were born in a time without much hope or trust, a time of concrete and comb-overs. It was an ugly time, buildings rising like bunkers, squatting gray and beige under hazy skies.

Your son was born in a year of permanent past tense, the year we found we had no future. Your son was born in the wake of a nightmare and lived no longer than a dream, and I could never tell if you were glad of this or not. I saw the photo on the mantel, a slight red thing in swaddling clothes. And I never really wanted to know. I thought to ask your ex-wife, but she wasn't online, wasn't anywhere at all where I could find her. I thought that was strange once, but no longer; no doubt you made a hungry hole in her life. No doubt you swallowed her up.

SWALLOW. Takes on the meaning "consume" or "destroy" after 1340. Cognate with the Old Norse *svelgr*, or "whirlpool." See also "devour."

THE RAIN IS ENDLESS and heavy with sludge, and the tree-tops are sagging and threatening to sink altogether under the onslaught. Days and days of being swept away: ark weather. But no ark this time. That's even what they're saying online: #noark. #wheresnoah. #endtimes.

It's always raining now, or always dry now. And all our days are like this now, here at the end of the world. Everything feels like a memory already. Everything feels like it's happening for the last time.

◆────────

PAREIDOLIA. Attaching significance to insignificant things. It's supposed to be an evolutionary advantage. We recognize human beings, can sort friend from foe. We make sense of a cluttered and chaotic world. We learn the shapes of the faces we love, learn to memorize the swollen tear-frown, the tilted smile. We memorize the sonnet of that strawberry hair.

◆────────

YOU PUT UP YOUR TOWER the year before the fire; your temple, you called it, and you documented its rise in riveting detail for your followers on Instagram. You said it should be like staring at the sun; the only way we have of seeing ghosts. It should be, you said, an afterimage tattooed on the soul. #Bullshit, I said, and you said the #endtimes was no place for #haters.

A massive structure, you forced your disciples to build it brick by brick. You decreed it be no less than fourteen stories tall, that the walls be enameled in your image: with bas-reliefs and murals made of precious stones, brightly colored and brilliant. Terra-cotta torches embedded in the plaster. Gold drains to keep out the rising waters. You spoke to the city of a place of peace, a place to lift our new god up to the heavens and to bury and renew our dreams. But like all the artisans, I saw the plans. I saw the great stone table at the top of the temple. I saw the smooth pit below, large enough to hold so many bodies. I saw the altar, strong enough to hold a human heart up, high enough to house a god.

I TEXTED YOU

> No
> No
> No
> **SRSLY NO STOP**

until you begged me to make your stupid crown, until you cajoled, until you finally came down from your dream to our old apartment on the outskirts of the city.

I was living there alone by then, surrounded by the things you had renounced and left behind. You'd come and gone in my life, just a few years together between your sorrows and your delusions. But now you wanted my artistry, and maybe, still, wanted me, too. Or at least I pretended so. No one else can make a crown fit for the gods, you said. We need you for our final glory.

And do you remember? How I laughed, how I sat down on the couch we bought at some old discount barn, ringed by brushes and paints untouched since you left me? I am no longer an artist, I told you, and you knelt before me and your hands were on me and your mouth was warm and your body was no god's, full of give and sag, and then you were moving underneath me like a man starving for love, just a man after all. But then after, you slipped on your robes and that ridiculous hat and you became a deity once more. You'll do it? you asked, You'll make the crown for me? and I understood then: this sex was never about love, never about your own body's need. It was about mine, and how you knew it would undo me in the end. It always has, this great need to melt the world in the flames of passion, to burn everything down behind me, even in the savage dream of these sorry times we inhabit.

BURN. A combined word from the Old Norse "to kindle" and the Old English "to be on fire." The later expression "to burn one's bridges" probably stems from the Civil War and a series of reckless cavalry raids. But in the end it was you who burned your bridges, not me—and then you were your own blaze. You died in the great fire that swept the floodwaters away, and your unfinished temple was consumed by the blaze like everything else.

———◄———————

LONG BEFORE THIS, before you asked a city to love you, it was just the two of us in our double bed by the barred window. We lay watching the shadows creep up the walls, and even with the bars and bricks I suddenly felt afraid. You turned to me, and your face was dark as the creepers, and you told me your son was returning to earth.

It is always this way, at the end of things, you said. The people will need a god.

Are you fucking kidding me, I said.

Same thing, you said, and kissed my forehead, chastely, like the saint you were becoming. I despised you when you got this way; I wanted to ask Herod for your head.

Your son, I started, then stopped because I did not wish to know. There are boxes better locked. And I shivered and wished you gone, even then. Already it was growing too hard to love a statue.

———◄———————

WE MET AT one of my shows, of course. The photographer you were with then fired off a few shots before heading for the free cocktails, and we were left alone. I'm a scientist, you told me. I study long-dead places.

I laughed and told you I was your opposite: I make new things and I never look back. You were long and lean, but not strong; you had a bruised, thin look about you. You stared at one of my sculptures, for an age it seemed, a gold and cold clay abstract, and finally I asked to share your night.

When you looked at me for the first time your gaze was a blue streak of sunlight—an impossibility, I know, but so bright and blue and warm I have no other way to say it.

I hope that will help explain why I stayed, when I never should have. I hope that will explain why I left you when you needed me most, in those red days when we hardly remembered the color blue at all.

———◆———

YOU INSISTED THAT your temple be dressed in blue: priests' robes dyed indigo, aqua for the eyes of the goddess figures set into nooks along the narrow passageways. You said the ancient Egyptians called blue the color of heaven. You said it looked great in pictures. #lapislazuli.

Your guard, henchman, thugs—whatever you'd call them, they roused me at midnight and brought me before you. My neighbor pounded on the walls in protest at the noise they made. I stood there before your temple, I refused you your blue and you grew angry, threatened the rack, the wheel. Seriously, the rack? I said. You'd grown so medieval in months. Would you have built them just for me? You said even I was not immune to the gods' wrath; I would not be protected forever. You stood at the top of your temple steps with your personal guard, their pistols cocked and at the ready, and I knelt down and prayed. I prayed to the god-that-was-you, O #shit-lord, to strike the memories from my skull, from our life before you rendered yourself ridiculous as a community theater pharaoh. I knelt for a very long time, until my knees went numb and my hands were half sunk in the fresh soil.

And when the sun sank, I looked up, and you were no longer there. You and your guard had disappeared in the dark, leaving me in my own blue night, alone.

———

THE LAST CHRISTMAS we spent with your sisters, the year before you went mad: in a drunken fit you poured your whiskey over the fire, shouted how we were *entitled* to paradise. Your sisters rolled their eyes at one another and laughed. They were always dark where you were fair, merry where you were serious, and you never could forgive them for it. (When you showed up to your temple ground-breaking with golden robes and a scepter, your eldest sister sent me this text: *LOL he's ALWAYS been a little emperor.*)

Later, after you'd opened a few presents and calmed the fuck down under the stockings and strings of rainbow lights, I said, I am totally okay here without paradise. Why can't you feel the same? Why can't you be content with the small things we have? Why can't you just stop your bitching?

You shook your head, ate a last bite of cookie. Crumbs in your mustache, you told me you could never be content here on earth. And I just smiled and took you in my arms, O fallen brilliance, eating cookies and drinking milk from a mug shaped like a reindeer's head. Your hair smelled like strawberry shampoo. I felt so sad and embarrassed for you, and so in love.

END. Usage in Old English meant death or destruction, the literal end. It wasn't until 1917 that we got "endtime," for the end of not just one thing but everything, #endofallthethings.

IN THIS DRY and poisoned time, the earth perished more quickly than we'd thought possible. With the bees went the plants, with the plants went the herbivores, with the herbivores went most of the carnivores, and they'd been going for so long we barely even registered their absence. For a short time, cattle remained: a great madness for beef infected the people of the cities, and for a while a simple hanger steak was more precious than a silo full of gold. We pretended to be sorry, to be horrified by our sudden and helpless desire for animal flesh; we blamed it on the shortage of protein, on the collapse of human civilization and our descent into primitivism. We blamed it on our children, O hungry mouths, and on the physical labor that was a growing part of our lives. We blamed it on #mcdonalds.

But it didn't matter. Soon the cows were gone, all of them, and we learned to make do with synthetics again. We ate freeze-dried meals sprinkled with pea protein mix. We ate without passion and without pleasure. We rolled the dry earth over our tongues and tried to remember the taste of honey, of chocolate, of salty pork and crisp, sweet apples. We dreamt of peaches, of peppers, of flaky fish and juicy tomatoes, and creamy avocado spooned over black beans and rice.

You laughed at the new cookbooks, the websites that sprang up offering recipes for fake foods. At the new chefs—food mimics, they called themselves—and the restaurants and food trucks they opened in the secret places of the city. You were starting to become just a little bit famous, your blog a watering hole for the city's conspiracy theorists. You were starting to make no sense, to speak in empty syllables, easier than the new food to digest and harder to make sense of. You said you were revolted by this stubborn tendency to cling to what we knew, to refuse the challenge of change.

Change? I asked.

Yes, you said. We are becoming something else, higher beings. We are purifying our bodies.

That night I refused to sleep with you. That was back

before you believed you were a deity, when you still wanted sex. Back when you thought it was good for the blood and the brain. Not tonight, I said, I am purifying my body. I smiled into my pillow.

That night I dreamed of a hot fudge sundae, topped with a perfect, fat maraschino cherry. You tossed and turned and worried about the blood flow to your brain while I swallowed vanilla ice cream, fast as my dream could churn it.

***

AND IT WASN'T UNTIL 1927 that we got "end" as in "finished," as in "the limit." As in "the last goddamn straw."

***

I FIRST FOUND the stranger stumbling over boxes in the basement. I was frightened; you were no longer living at home and he was a big man, though starved and exhausted. He said he was only looking for food, as so many were, but I didn't like the cruel circles under his eyes. They looked like coal thumbprints.

He's a useful man, you said, when I brought him to you, and I didn't like the way you said it. You'd grown thinner and mysterious, living in the foundations of your temple, and you stopped sleeping with me altogether, coming home only to hole up in the back bedroom with your laptop and your voice recorder.

At first I wondered what you wanted him for, this stranger. For love? For friendship? To be another of your disciples? I remembered the way you turned to me, months ago, during a commercial for #syntheticgardens, and told me that I was your acolyte. You said it the way normal people say "baby" or "sweetheart."

The stranger took the back bedroom, and when you came back you would spend hours in there with him, both of your eyes shining with zealotry when you emerged. I still thought I could cure you back then, so I let it happen, I let him stay and let you preach to him and make him yours. I knew you thought he was your son come back to you and I let it happen. I admit it, even now, I was happy to let him take on the duties I didn't care to assume. To be your acolyte. I thought that if he was, perhaps then I could be your wife once more.

———

You and he began with flyers, but as our poor dying city flocked to you and filled your coffers, you graduated to a website, to email lists, to gathering fans and followers and building an online army. You posted pictures of your temple's progress on your website, next to a thermometer and a button that said DONATE. You were a serious sort of joke, a cheap gamble for many desperate souls.

HELP A NEW WORLD SWIM ASHORE, your subject line read, and yes, yes, I signed up for your goddamn email list. How could I not? I was following every second of this train wreck with my opera glasses; I was waiting for this new world to swim ashore like some Toho terror and stamp us all out. You included.

·——————

APOPHENIA. The human tendency to seek patterns in random nature, where there are no patterns to be found. See also: ghosts, gambling, and the passions of religious mania and prophecy. See also: what happens when your lover's brain breaks down while the world is burning.

I was born the day they found a face on Mars. It was a lie, of course; it was a geographical anomaly, a trick of the terrain. We want so badly to make sense of the cosmos, to see it in ourselves. We turn shadows into sockets, bright smears into mouths and eyes.

We turn the universe into our mirror. #narcissus, naturally.

·——————

WE THREE AT the budding temple: you would map the fires, chart them out on a complicated grid. You said it showed how the world would end. And when. You painted strange symbols on the spreading gold of your floor. And the stranger would help you, connecting the dots with indigo while you made phone calls like a politician, raising money for your shrine. The stranger would stare at me with those shiny eyes, those sugar-glazed membranes, and I thought then that I would burn, too.

IN OUR LIFE TOGETHER, we loved jazz and swing, especially Ellington. We would dance to "Come to Baby, Do!" and you would sing along, crooning softly into my ear. Moonlight and streetlights and the low hum of love, and you were as bright and handsome as a satellite. Was it any wonder I orbited you, was your companion star?

Your name before you changed it: a fusty yet furious string of syllables, Old Europe braided with the raw spirit of the New World.

Your name after you changed it: the dead name of a lost god, buried ten thousand years ago under a swollen, ancient sun. You said it meant the son of Ra.

But what's in a name? Or so you said, what seems like ages ago now. What's in a name, indeed, and so I started calling you Junior instead. Online I took shit from your followers for #junior-ing you. But in petty times like these, we must do what we can to keep our hurts at bay. We must take our tiny revenges.

THE STRANGER, you said, was a healer. In just a year, you said, he'd healed: One woman with six toes on each foot, one child with tuberculosis, one blind man, three people with the avian flu, one snake and two turtles burned at a reptile house, one child with a clubfoot, one child with a cleft palate, one grown man with shingles, sixteen people with various cancers, and seven barren women.

———

WE WOULD SIT BY the fire, always the three of us now, always his glassy eyes on me. Women find him very attractive, you told me, and it was true: his face had a certain ascetic beauty, all sharp cheekbones and razor eyes.

The stranger said very little. I asked him why, once, and he told me words had ever been a bane to him, had ever led him into trouble and damnation. Your man saved me, he said, and I have eyes to thank him. And ears to hear his prayers. That is enough.

And hands and a mouth and other things besides, I said to myself, thinking of those barren women. Pretty and young and plump, all of them, like sows led to breeding. I wondered how their husbands felt; if they were glad of the "miracle" or ashamed to warrant another man's assistance, no matter how holy. And what, at the end of the world, were we breeding more mouths for?

I hated the stranger; to me he was a wild animal, a rooting boar, and I was sorry you had decided to use him so. I wondered if he would turn on you, or me, or get free before that could happen.

But *you* turned on me instead. *You* offered me to

75

him. *You* said it was necessary, that you were now as a god and he your earthly representative—that this sacrifice was needed to make the fields fertile again. You said these things and I stared, white and crimson, and if someone had given me a weapon I would have sacrificed something, oh yes. I would have cut off your balls with a butter knife just then. I would have held you down for as long as it took, stuffed you between your own teeth like a #humanhogroast. You saw my fury and said we would speak no more of it, and then you made me tea, and when I awoke I was laid out like a cross in the back bedroom. I was draped over the blankets and my clothes were gone and so were his and he was smiling all plastic and coming toward me and the world was on fire but you were calmly chanting and suddenly I heard the words, under all this madness you were sing-chanting Ellington, you were singing, "So, pucker up, my sweet, and meet your Waterloo, come to baby, do!"

And then I screamed and screamed and screamed and I think I would have screamed forever had the stranger not slapped my face. You scowled at him, called me the mother of all life, said be respectful for fuck's sake, and I gaped and gasped and dragged the blankets over my breasts, and with a sudden strength I didn't know I had, I changed my trajectory. I shot out of orbit, renegade star, I packed my things and made for the Motel 6 on the other side of town and all the while I heard "Come to baby, do!" like a spell through my brain and I spat at it, I wept over it, and I drowned it with music and booze and dice and sleep. And I drowned it deep in sweet red fire.

◄———————

Moon. Face notwithstanding, the moon is a source of madness just the same. Or so say the police, hospital staff, and good old Pliny the Elder, who theorized that perhaps humans were so affected by the moon because they—like the tides—were made mostly of water, especially the brain. The full moon, in particular, is believed to hand us lunatics, werewolves, and criminals. The moon reaches down with silver fingers and toys with us; and we reach up and destroy the moon.

◄———————

THE NIGHT YOUR temple burned down—arson, it was whispered—it was my birthday, and I felt the full moon breathing down my neck as I remembered I was circling the world without you now. The stranger had burned with you—your son, they said, this news was trending—and they called you a madman. They seethed, but understood—how false words were part of the new darkness. They understood how easy it was to become a prophet, #endtimesscamartist, how easy it was to sow hope among the hopeless.

At your funeral—held like those of the kings of

old, your pyre signaling only the absence of a body—I wore my bluest dress and wondered if there really was a world beyond. There was a feeling of bacchanalia in the room, your worshippers mentally popping champagne corks and dancing in frenzies. It seemed possible to see a kind of heaven in their stares, a cruel human dream of heaven. And I did not forgive you.

In Which Athena Designs a Video Game with the Express Purpose of Trolling Her Father

———————➤

IN THIS ONE, SHE TELLS ZEUS, YOU HAVE TO SAVE THE HUMAN world from a vengeful god.

Mmm, he says. He is eating a cheeseburger in bed, watching college basketball and only half-listening. Mustard hangs in his beard here and there, gold on white. She dabs at the spots, her lovely face shifting slightly with something more godlike than disgust.

You can play as one of three nymphs, she says.

Nice, he says. Zeus is really into nymphs.

It's open-world, Athena tells him. There are all kinds of side quests and mini-games, beauty contests and drowned-sailor-saving and whatnot. But the main point of the game is to avoid this one specific god until you're powerful enough, because if you run into him before then, you'll get turned into a cow or a tree.

That sucks, says Zeus. Can you drink a potion or something to turn you back? Find a magical object?

No potion, says Athena, but you can still play through as a cow or a tree.

That's good, says Zeus. WHAT! Did you see that foul? HOW DID THEY NOT CALL THAT FOUL? The bed shakes, and snaking fissures appear on the TV screen.

Jesus, Dad, says Athena. Did you take your pills? Your blood pressure.

I did, honey, it's fine, says Zeus. I'm fine. Tell me more about your game. I'm listening. He leans back, eyes on the screen.

Well, she says, if you really want to punish yourself, you can start as a cow and play the whole thing like that. It's the advanced mode. Europa Mode, I call it.

Zeus narrows his eyes. Athena waits. Trolling Zeus is dangerous, after all. Last time Hera did it, he turned her into an earthworm for a year.

Finally, he nods. Go ahead, he says. Put it into production.

She breathes, adjusts her diadem. She starts off to hire developers. Just wait until he sees the way he looks in game, foolish and flaccid.

WAIT, says the Father of Gods. His shout splits the television. Crack. Sizzle. The stink of singed wires.

Athena stops, halfway through dematerializing. She wonders what it feels like to eat nothing but earth for a year. She really enjoys mortal foods, and wine, and mortal men and women, too. She grips her staff. Yes?

Make sure all the nymphs have big tits, says Zeus. A little fanservice, you know?

Athena nods, rolls her eyes, dissolves. Her godlike disappointment lags behind, a cold blue cloud, and Zeus wonders why he feels so weird and so goddamned small.

He grabs his phone and texts Hephaestus: *hey kiddo, need a new tv. big. make it happen plz.* He waits, then texts again: *r u watching this game? miss u,* as plaintive and lonely and punctuationally awkward as any dad on earth.

Is the Future a
Nice Place for Girls

---------------►

THE QUEEN WOKE UP ONE MORNING TO THE FURIOUS SOUND
of the Future invading. It had that rumbling, insistent
sound all uprisings carry with them.

The king was still sleeping, his heavy body a wide
lump under the damask. The guards, used to his snor-
ing, were all half-asleep too. The queen poked him,
gently then not-so-gently, shouting until he snorted
himself awake.

What the hell, he said. I need my royal rest.

It's the Future, the queen told him, ears tilted toward
the commotion outside. Don't you hear it? It's coming,
and fast, and we need to flee. She could hear screams,
shouts, the sickening sound of bodies crashing into new
ideas. She could hear speeches being made. She could
hear the present coming apart.

We're not going anywhere, said the king. The Future
doesn't frighten me. My guards will take care of it.

I don't think they will, said the queen. She heard another thud, then the distinct sound of bone crunching. I don't think they are.

Well, I'm not going anywhere, said the king. And I don't hear anything, anyway. I think you're mad.

Fine, said the queen. She'd always strongly disliked the king, forced into the marriage after her elder sister disgraced the family by having secret and robust babies with a shepherd. You should do the same, she told her younger sister, just before she was hauled off to the nunnery. The breeding stock is so much better.

The queen got dressed, quickly, all by herself, and some things were assuredly on backwards or sideways but she didn't care. She ran to the nursery where her infant daughter was sleeping and began to swaddle her.

Your Majesty, said the wet nurse, shocked. What are you doing?

The Future is coming for us, so we're leaving, said the queen. Come on, Matilda. You come too.

It's Alice, said the wet nurse. And I'm not leaving! What a dreadful thought.

Fine, said the queen. She packed a few of the baby's things in a small velvet bag and she ran. She could hear the clang of the spears, the scrape of the pickaxes, the news anchors broadcasting, the rumbling of engines. The Future forcing its way in.

Once outside, she could hear the castle gates opening—it was surrendering to the Future. Fine, she thought. I'll slip right through. She ran just in time to avoid a stream of cars weaving about, the drivers and passengers hitting frantic sheep and pigs in their distraction. They were all gazing up, dazzled by the turrets and by the great north tower, with its spire of beaten gold. More people were holding up guidebooks, or looking down at phones, charging into knights who then lay on the pavement with their lances shattered, moaning and invisible.

This is where they cut off the king's head, the queen heard, and she held the baby's wobbly head with one hand and picked up her skirts with the other. How had they missed the signs? The Future never arrived suddenly. It was always anticipated, announced. There were omens. How could their seer have failed to see?

The queen jogged on, unused to the exertion but determined to survive. The baby, lulled by the motion, was quieted. She slept. The queen passed trams, trampled fields, serfs standing mournfully next to slaughtered oxen, and curious tourists in yellow wellies. Men with large guns were pointing them everywhere, taking down pheasants and peasants with equal aplomb. Nobody recognized her, thank goodness; her cloak and the chaos guaranteed her some brief anonymity.

She stopped, finally, at a tavern in the next town over, exhausted and in need of a bed and some food. She asked the barman for some milk for the baby. Skim or whole? he asked, and she stared. Never mind, he said, I think whole is what babies drink. The queen put a little on her finger, and let the baby suck it off. The child had a dozy little face, big bleary brown eyes, and the queen was quite in love with it. The child was already betrothed to the Duke of Something or Other; a young man known for his unexceptional face and exceptional cruelty, but perhaps (she hoped) he hadn't escaped the Future. She sighed and turned to the woman next to her, shockingly muscular and got up in breeches.

Is the Future a nice place for girls, the queen asked, and the fit woman snorted. Not exactly, she said. But— and she eyed the queen's cloak and shoes and hair— better than where you come from.

Thank goodness, said the queen, and she kissed her daughter's slack fat cheeks, her fuzzy head. She held the baby carefully as she hauled herself up onto the barstool, the cool indifference of the barman an astonishing relief. No one was looking at her. The air was thick with conversation. This is the Future, she told her daughter. The baby opened her eyes and looked around.

Our Mutual (Theater) Friend

———————————————◆

THE PROBLEM, IN PLAIN TERMS: SHE ONCE WAS AN ACTRESS. Even in younger years she played the boozy diva—hovering in the wings, faintly sardonic—until the crucial point in the musical when she took over the stage and sang the big, sizzling, fourth-wall-shattering solo number that exposed the hypocrisy and artifice of the whole show. Audiences loved her; directors loved her; reviewers loved her. No matter how little stage time she got, she was always the main draw and the de facto star.

The problem, in plainer terms: she still thinks of herself as an actress. She hasn't acted for many years, retiring early after a disastrous marriage and a quiet breakdown. But she still hangs out in the metaphorical wings, drinking too much and expounding on life with a level of wit inappropriate to shopping for shoes at Nordstrom Rack. She explodes every now and then in the most embarrassing fashion, usually at children's birthday parties. She doesn't sing—thank god!—but her dramatic speech patterns at these moments rival Norma Desmond's and confuse her friends' small children, who have never seen golden-age cinema or Sondheim. During the latest outburst, she waxes on at Brooklyn Davis's fourth birthday party ("for a good goddamn ten minutes," claims Brooklyn Davis's father) about the vulgarity of modern pizza parlors, upstaging Elmo and Abby and Cookie Monster—not to mention the pirate-themed face painters. Their mutual friends convene the next day at the dog park, positive it's time to take action.

Marcus's birthday is next Saturday, says Pam Perkins. And we rented a bounce house. It cost a *fortune*, she says.

And she's supposed to be seeing *Hamilton* with Jack and me the weekend after, says Jenny Jackson. Jenny and Jack are child-free, and feel unfairly saddled with their eccentric friend whenever they head to the movies or the theater. God knows, says Jenny darkly, what she'll think of the show or when she'll decide to stand up and say it.

She seems so unhappy, says Anna Lowenstein. I want to help but—

But when you ask about her life, says Aisha Rollins, all you get is a weird, albeit witty, retort.

Exactly, says Jonathan Yan. She called me "my dull darling" in front of the waiter at Shake Shack the other day.

The others nod; it can't go on. Indeed, it's getting worse. Her outbursts were once rare, and only at dinner parties and diners late at night. But she seems to have an opinion almost every day now, and she chooses her moments carefully, gathering drama and timing to her like a very loud dress.

She needs an audience again, says someone, but none of *them* have said it. They turn around and there on the park bench is a very old man: brown teeth, white hair, skin like an old saddle. He laughs. Aisha Rollins glares.

Your friend needs an audience, he says again, and Jonathan shakes his head. She'll never sing again, says Jonathan. She's lost the voice. It's part of the problem.

The old man laughs. Doesn't need a voice to have an audience, he says. Just needs this. His voice is congested, tubercular, and Jenny moves away just slightly. He hands Jonathan a small glass ball, a snow globe with no snow. Inside, a tiny wooden theater stage sits, apron empty, curtain down, tiny people sitting at the edge of tiny seats. Something about it speaks of waiting, of a deep, long hush. All the friends stare into it, hushed and caught up in the waiting, too.

Give it to her, says the old man. As a gift. And then he's gone, the air strangely still where he stood a moment ago. They blink, the sun in their eyes after the cool dark of the miniature theater.

I bet he doesn't even have a dog, says Anna. What a weirdo, they all agree with relief.

But then they gift it to her anyway, for reasons none of them quite understand.

Jonathan is her favorite—they were briefly lovers, long before he married his husband—and he makes the trek to deliver it. Her studio apartment is tragic because it is nothing like appropriate to her outsized personality and fading star persona. The blinds are dusty and off-white, the carpets are beige, the furniture is flawed Pottery Barn, purchased ages ago at a warehouse sale.

Come in, darling, she says, as always. She is pretending to work when he knocks, and she goes right back to it after she lets him in. Pounding away at a computer keyboard, for chrissakes she has no idea how to type. She's claimed for ages to be freelancing, though she never says what for and anyway everyone knows she got a fat settlement when she divorced her broker husband.

Jonathan hands her the globe. She looks at it, her eyes watering, her ashtray full. Her hands are still beautiful, translucent as they catch the soft light inside the thing. Enjoy it, he says, and then he does the strangest thing—he runs. He'll tell his husband later he has no idea why, a middle-aged man running down four flights of stairs and into traffic like a lunatic. But really, he runs because he sees her face as she holds it; that glow and that head tilt and that proud eye pure Gloria Swanson, and he does not want to see what happens next.

What happens next: she doesn't show up for Marcus's bounce-house birthday, and she fails to keep her theater date with Jenny and Jack. She doesn't call, and she doesn't text, and she doesn't write, and she doesn't answer her door. She doesn't show up at Nordstrom Rack, or at Macy's, or at any of her shopping haunts. She doesn't opine, anywhere, on anything.

Anna and Jonathan finally convince her landlord to let them in. The landlord sniffs, disgust pulling his mouth down. He's sure she's probably a corpse, but there's no body anywhere. Only an overturned Pottery Barn wicker chair, the familiar garnet walls hung with gilt-framed show posters, the steam radiators draped with her wet clothing since she never bothered to get a dryer. Jonathan goes looking, hands and knees, for the globe. He's sure—quite unexpectedly—of where she is. He wonders how he'll square his previously practical worldview with what he finds. He sees the glint of glass near the sofa, shouts for Anna. He closes his eyes, opens them. Looks.

But he sees only glass shards and glitter, a few plastic seats and stage fragments scattered over the beige carpet. Their friend is nowhere here, and he and Anna pick up glass and try not to cut their hands on this dreadfully stupid illusion.

The Dry Cleaner from
Des Moines

I N LAS VEGAS, THE WOMAN HAD FOUND THE KIND OF LUCK she liked best.

Her best luck involved invisibility, the kind that allowed people to overlook her sticky fingers and her quiet dine-and-dashes. She was tan and brown and beige and gray, plain and unobtrusive as backdrop. She wasn't offensive or even unattractive. Just the one person in the bar you'd pass over as you scanned the potential pickings. The one you couldn't ID in a police lineup.

Her plainness had been a source of some small pain in her youth; often, she would wonder if she'd ever find love, ever cash in her virginity. Eventually, the disappointment of loneliness gave way to a kind of exhilaration, the understanding that she alone possessed a sort of superpower. As long as she was careful and committed only small crimes, and carried a little luck with her, she could do more or less as she liked.

When she ordered drinks, she chose what was on tap and didn't linger long—she kept her face blank and drank briskly, though not quickly enough to arouse attention. She sidled off the barstool and strolled out calmly, and often the empty glass left behind was the only way anyone knew she'd been there. In stores, she could pocket things and stroll right out—even when they had camera footage, she was so nondescript the police just shook their heads. She looked, they said, like anyone's mother. How on earth would they find her?

She moved around a lot, never stayed in one neighborhood long. It was always cities and suburbs, because there she never stood out; so many invisible people haunt the shops and strip malls of suburban America. And now she found herself in Las Vegas, unwilling to leave though she'd surely outstayed her welcome by now. Her luck had just been too good.

She was, she thought, the only person in Vegas who wasn't there to gamble (though she supposed what she was doing was a version of that) or drink or marry. Or, she corrected herself, to do business; Vegas these days had a whole sideline in conventions and meetings, full as it was of large, cheap hotels and plenty of diversion. She was also, she thought, the only person who actually liked the Strip, but not because it was the Strip. She liked it because of what she became inside it. The grandiose, improbable casinos, competing with one another for pomp versus circumstance, flashing marquis desire versus plaster Paris and Rome. It was all so impossibly large and complex and so well-oiled that a person like her could disappear inside, a plain little pinball pinging around inside a neon nerve network.

She spent her days wandering the false streets of Venice, the plaza of Rome, the Eiffel Tower. She sat with a drink sometimes, watched countless strangers win and lose more money than she'd ever have—sometimes skillfully, sometimes not. Luck, she thought, featured into most winning, but there was also a small group of almost invisible people—invisible like her—and you'd never know it to look at them, but they were the real geniuses at winning. At poker. At blackjack. Some even worked the slots. They were never flashy, or loud, or overconfident. None of them looked like James Bond. They wore faded sweatshirts, cargo shorts, reading glasses, cropped hair. They were quiet, and she knew their secrets only because she'd seen them winning, over and over again. She noticed the special little privileges they had: large sums advanced to them, access to special rooms, complimentary drinks, and exaggerated deference from the casino staff. All of it small, unobtrusive, hushed as aristocracy and real, serious money.

If she'd been a different sort of criminal, she'd have tried to become one of them, imitate or impersonate them. But she couldn't; there was nothing to grasp, no detail substantial or solid. The regulars were like ghosts. They haunted the places reliably, but beyond their scheduled appearances they were silent and secretive, and anything left of their lives before had been buried.

One late afternoon, she was pocketing soap at a fancy bath store in the Venetian, and a shadow fell over her shoulder. She was ready; she arranged her expression in blank, neutral confusion. She turned. It was one of the regulars, a shorter man in a blue polo and khaki shorts. His hair was in a graying brown ponytail. His face was so unremarkable it was almost a blur. Just like her. She had seen him winning big at the craps tables at the MGM Grand. Yes? she said.

If you want to cheat, he said, go high-stakes. It's Vegas! Why steal bath bombs? His voice was louder than she'd expected it would be.

She raised one eyebrow. Excuse me, I'm not stealing anything, she said. You must be mistaken. He put his hand in her jeans pocket (her front pocket, the *nerve*) and pulled out a thirty-dollar soap shaped like a scalloped cupcake. She raised her other eyebrow. The store clerk started toward them and she took it to the counter, furious. The bath she took with this strawberry-scented soap might be perfectly pleasant, but it would not be worth thirty dollars. Her hands shook as she counted out bills, saw the gambler was still standing there, watching her. She was usually cool as milk.

I've seen you, he said, walking out, following fast on her sensible heels. MGM Grand. Harrods. Caesars. I've seen you pretending to play the slots. What are you really doing here? Not just petty theft, I assume.

You've never seen me, she said, walking faster. How had he seen her? No one did. Her heart fluttered and people stared. Her face felt flooded with spotlight.

I used to be a dry cleaner, he said. From Des Moines. But I see everything. I notice everything. Always have. Had an eye for stains, the small stuff nobody else sees. That's how I came to be a gambler instead of a dry cleaner. Followed my heart, came out here. What's your passion? I'm staying at the Venetian. I like it here—I like the way the ceiling is a sky, how you can think you're somewhere cool and breezy. I like the gold things, everywhere. I like gold. They call me Midas at the MGM, I've won so often. What's your name? Where are you staying?

Nowhere, she said, frowning. She reminded herself to be a blank. She was staying at the Mirage and that was much too close to him, just across the street—and anyway she'd have to skip town tonight, get on a bus and bail. She was even angrier at the thought. She *liked* Vegas. She wanted to *stay* here. Her sensible, invisible shoes clacked loudly on the Venetian walkway tiles, and she glared at the gondoliers, who seemed suddenly poised to offer her a ride.

Who was this man and why had he ruined her superpower?

Let's get a pizza, he said, and grabbed her arm. Or a cookie. There's a great Hawaiian cookie place. I want to talk to you. I think you're fascinating. I'd love to sleep with you. She stopped. I'll turn you in, he said playfully, then put his hand over hers. This was the second time he'd touched her, and it was a sensation she was utterly unused to. Her insides curled.

The long con, she thought. He'd be such a perfect mark. She could take, and take, and take, and one day disappear. But she wasn't made for the long con. She was made for minute-crime, for in and out and gone. What would happen if he could see her, even just for a night? Would it break some spell? Render her features more distinct, her outline suddenly pulled into a fixed shape?

On the Greyhound to Reno, the man next to her mumbled to himself for a while and fell asleep. He smelled like whiskey and sour smoke. The teenager behind her hit her with his rucksack, and seemed to wonder who he was apologizing to. The bus driver tried to focus on her and failed, squeezing himself behind the wheel and dreaming about his shift end, his Xbox and a cold Bud Light. She leaned back in her seat and sighed. She called the police on the burner phone, told them where to find a lot of recently stolen goods—the thief in room 1205. The Mirage. Hurry, he's probably still asleep. How did she know? Didn't want to say. He might be dangerous, careful now.

She'd be more careful from now on. Her luck was made, not found; this she now knew. She tossed the phone out the window and waited for the bus to grind on out of this McDonald's parking lot, gravel spitting, wheels rolling toward the next big town to take her out of focus.

The Eyes of Saint Lucy

B ECAUSE THERE IS NO GOD, MY MOTHER ONCE MARRIED A
man named Arnie Barney.

Arnie owned a shooting range in Gary with a badly
stuffed bear on the roof. The shooting range was called,
confusingly, Barney's Bear Range; it was assumed Arnie
acquired the bear before the shooting range, though
no curious party was ever able to ask him—he died six
months into the marriage of a massive coronary. My
young mother Wendy inherited the shooting range,
which took in just enough to keep her above water until
she met my father. She did not take the bear when she
sold the business, though she told me much later she
used to climb up and talk to him when she got lonely.

My mother's second husband, and my father, was
only somewhat more reasonably named Hollis Barcus.
The newly christened Wendy Barcus, besotted with martyrs and medieval saints, married a thoroughly modern

man who'd martyred himself to that twentieth-century tyrant, time. Wendy made space and stillness, Hollis made lists and timetables. It stood to reason the marriage would be troubled.

But why Hollis? Why Wendy? Why the two together?

WHAT HOLLIS TOLD US:
1. When he was young and single, Hollis drove by the shooting range every day on his way to work, and often saw my mother up on the roof with that bear.
2. He started to think of her like King Kong's Fay Wray, floating dresses and flying hair alongside that misshapen creature. He began to wonder if she was just a vision, if he was going mad. He began to wonder if he could rescue her.
3. Hollis left his home twenty-two minutes early one morning, and pulled his car off the highway and into the shooting range parking lot.
4. Would you like to have coffee with me, he shouted up to my mother.
5. What? shouted my mother.
6. Hollis Barcus, twenty-five and in very good shape (fifty push-ups every morning immediately on waking), decided to climb. He clambered up the drainpipe, shimmied up the shingles, and hoisted himself onto the hot

flat part of the roof. He felt very pleased with himself—especially when my mother turned out to be young and beautiful and somewhat substantial—and he decided to fall in love with her.

———

WHAT MY MOTHER TOLD US:

1. She was up there on the roof, green blanket spread over beige shingles, conversing with the bear like she did many mornings. Sometimes she told him stories. Sometimes she prayed, though she didn't exactly believe in a benevolent god. Hers was an angry god, furious and disapproving, and she prayed mostly for revenges and disappointments. She prayed to be martyred in briefly agonizing ways.

2. Sometimes she prayed that the bear would spring to life and eat her; she was so very lonely. Her parents—my grandparents—had died in a car accident when she was only a teenager, and she met Arnie Barney when she was just eighteen, turning down his bed at a small motel in Muncie. He was running a booth at a gun show, and she hated guns, my mother. But she hated being lonely and poor even more.

3. She wasn't sad when Arnie died. He was

middle-aged and purplish and had acne all
over his back. He used to weep involuntarily
when they made love. It made the bile rise in
my mother's throat. She often prayed they
wouldn't have a child.

4. Hollis Barcus was handsome, young, and literally climbing a building to rescue my mother.

5. She thought he was an idiot, also, because he
   didn't use the ladder propped up against the
   siding.

6. But a handsome and enterprising idiot, and
   anyway prayers didn't always turn out exactly
   the way one intended. That was the problem
   with prayer.

———————

BOTH OF THESE VERSIONS could be true, and not true, but
the facts remain in place: Hollis took Wendy on twenty-
minute dates; he learned the fastest route to her little
apartment in Gary; he promised her a big diamond and
delivered in full; he made the payments from their joint
bank account on the 16th at precisely 12:15 p.m. every
month for two years without fail. He moved her to
Muncie and bought her a home in the suburbs.

Also true: after making do for so many years on
her own, my mother was exhausted. She was a young
woman with the heart of an old widow. An upside-down
fairy tale. She wanted:

1. To stop working.
2. To have children.
3. To buy a home.
4. To pray in quiet places.
5. To take up painting.
6. To be left alone.

Hollis, the efficiency expert, was good at leaving people alone. He performed his husbandly duties twice a week for ten minutes each, ate Wendy's mediocre meals every day for breakfast and dinner, and otherwise maximized his time elsewhere. He loved my mother, of course, in an abstract way, but the men and women in our neighborhood didn't spend much time in each other's company, and that was just the way things were. Hollis went bowling with his coworkers. My mother snubbed the neighbor ladies and their Tupperware parties to make dioramas of martyred saints. She didn't gossip with Mrs. Wagner, or play bridge with Mrs. Kowalczyk and her friends. When she was pregnant with my oldest brother, she didn't go to the birthing class that all the neighbor ladies went to at St. Anthony's. My two brothers were born healthy just the same, and spent their time brawling with other neighborhood boys in our little cul-de-sac.

This time may or may not have been fulfilling for Wendy, but I think she was happy enough in her way. She wasn't shouting her hopes and dreams over the sounds of gunshots, to a bear on a roof. She wasn't cleaning toilets or selling soap door-to-door or dropping newspapers off at four in the morning on doorsteps. She was a housewife and mother, and I think that's what she really wanted. Time to fill and then eventually, us to help her fill it, me and Feral Boy.

———◆———

IF THIS WERE A NORMAL family tale, here is where I would sketch for you a shape, foreshadow, or just flat out draw a character creeping his way into the story. I would tell you about the first time I fell in love with Feral Boy, and how it was confusing because his eyes were gray-gold and he smelled like wild sage but he was supposed to be my brother. I would tell you how it was even more confusing because everyone should have been a little in love with Feral Boy, he was so beautiful and lost. Perhaps I would start at the end, and tell you that he stars in movies now, and I still love him from far away. Perhaps I would start in the middle and tell you that somewhere in the years of protecting him and hating him, I fell to finding him a hurt flower, a fragile thing. And that resentment fell away at that. Or perhaps I would start at the beginning, with his scraped knees and messy hair and the stricken look on Wendy's face when Hollis brought him home.

But this is not a normal family story. Things will happen out of sequence, because this is a family out of sequence. Lists will be made, dreams will be probed, jokes will be listed in alphabetical order. And the Feral Boy will climb into this story just like he climbed into my window late at night: when it was time, when it was time, when it was the right delicious time.

I WAS WENDY'S LAST-BORN and I fought my birth, clawing my way out like a baby tiger. Fierce, blood-caked, defiant—I was destined, my mother said, to be fey.

My older brothers allowed me to tag along, useless little girl, until I was tough as they were. They taught me how to make a potato launcher, how to throw curveballs, how to throw a punch (thumb on the outside), how to swear like one of the shop foremen Hollis sometimes brought home to dinner. They taught me other things, too: how to cheat at Scrabble and Sorry! and Life, how to put a penny on the tracks and watch the train flatten it, how to blow a bubble big enough to pop, how to whistle, how to lie.

Most mothers would balance this out, teach their girls to wear dresses, throw tea parties. But Wendy wasn't really interested in those things.

Wendy, by the time I came along, had more or less sworn off sex, so I was a nearly holy miracle. She had become an ascetic of the suburban sort; she still poured a little whiskey into her tea and wore pastel capri pants and chain-smoked, but she also thought a lot—an overwhelming lot, she told me—about hell. Some days she'd keep me home from school to help her make her martyred saint dioramas, or pose for paintings of Saint Lucy or Saint Joan. She said with my big dark eyes I looked just like the girl in the film, gaze tilted heavenward, beatific in saintly suffering.

And she talked to me. She opened her mouth and

confessed her life in full, her parents and her childhood and the martyred lady saints and how she admired them so. Men she had no use for, not the saints or popes or even Jesus himself. She loved Mary like the sun, though, and she always wore the Virgin in a locket around her skinny neck.

Men are no good, Wendy often told me. You can't trust a single one.

Not even my brothers? I asked.

Not even them, said Wendy. They'll grow into men eventually.

Not even Hollis? I asked.

At that, she closed her mouth to me. Her eyes went small with something, but I couldn't see what. Times like that, you knew to stop asking questions. I watched her lick the tip of her paintbrush, acrylic scarlet streaks across her chin like blood.

Despite my spending so much time with her, Wendy was a ghost. She never had that solid feel, that reassuring weight of other kids' mothers. Hollis used to call her Sister Wendy, but I always thought of her remove as more unscripted than liturgy, more faery than faithful. So far as I could tell, her religion had mostly to do with martyred saints and mystics, with women married to an unseen world.

Wendy had no need or desire for good little girls, only holy ones, which wasn't quite the same. So I chose to live in her world, mostly. Somehow since birth I always knew this was my choice to make. I was wild, I was smart but impetuous, and possessed of a morbid

collection of knowledge about torture and religious suffering. I understood Hollis, and his need for order, his
love of modern things—but I chose to belong fully to
my mother. Hollis was never somehow serious enough,
you see, somehow always superficial in a way that
offended me deeply. At dinner he would tell us stories,
about him and my mother mostly, and he loved to tell
jokes, though he labored to tell them. He wasn't funny,
Hollis, though you could tell he longed to be. He was
just too punctual. Poor Hollis. So rational, so logical,
so terribly male in the blandest, prettiest way. He was
always behaving badly, though everyone thought I was
too young to notice. He was having affairs—very effi-
cient affairs—with several of the secretaries at Western Auto Parts Inc., and my mother was pretending not
to notice. You might think that dry, sober Hollis was
hardly the type, but my goodness, who better? Passion,
indiscretion—these never factored in. Hollis kept his
door locked and his stopwatch on, and though it made
the women giggle, it got to be a sort of thing at Western
Auto Parts Inc. Nobody quite knew if it was true—did
he really keep a timer? The women who knew for sure
weren't saying.

Wendy told me some years later that he only did it
because he could get away with it, and not because he
didn't love her. I think he thought it was something a
real person might do, she said. Hollis was very concerned
about trying to be a real person.

Oh, I know, I said. Hollis and I had that much in common. We were two people trapped in a strange dream,

trying to behave from time to time as though we weren't. For me it wasn't so bad—I'd been born into the dream, after all. But Hollis, well. Hollis got a stopwatch for his sixth birthday, and ever since, he'd been obsessed with time. Not time as a concept, or time as in: running out of. Rather, time split up, allotted, doled out. Time parsed and measured. Time served.

One minute fifteen seconds: the length of time Hollis could hold his breath. (He had asthmatic lungs.)

One minute thirty-two seconds: the length of time it took him to brush his teeth (thoroughly and carefully).

One minute forty-three seconds: the length of time he could go without thinking about Julie Connor for that one long month in fourth grade before she moved to Lincoln.

Two minutes ten seconds: the length of time he thought his time was up after he fell through the ice on the lake in early spring.

Twenty-four hours: the length of time he was grounded after going out on the lake to play hockey after he'd been told not to.

One week: the length of time his coach kept him benched on the football team after he and his friends were caught stealing lawn ornaments from Mrs. Murphy's Nativity display.

Eight months and fourteen days: the length of time Hollis took getting over the death of his high school sweetheart/chemistry teacher, Rolanda May, whom he was dating secretly.

Three years and nine months: the length of time it took Hollis to graduate from the University of Nebraska at Omaha with a degree in business management.

Four years and six months: the length of time it took Hollis to work his way up the chain of command at Western Auto Parts Inc. to become the assistant regional manager.

Eight years and six months: the length of time Hollis and my mother were married before he first started cheating on her.

Twenty years and four months: the length of time Hollis and my mother were married before she put cyanide in his coffee.

Someday, this studio will be mine. I've memorized it.
I've come to love it drearily, in the way I suppose you'd
find love in an arranged marriage, or a secondhand dress
you didn't pick out. Would you like the official tour? I get
my stillness and strangeness from Wendy, but like Hollis
I am a guide, an organizer. I gather, weave, divvy, and
make a path for making meaning, through the detritus
of Wendy's faith and mine. I'll show you what I mean.

We enter the small room through a plain wooden
door—notice the strong smell? The artist burns holy
incense—or, what she has purchased at the local head
shop and deemed to be holy incense—whenever she is at
work in her studio. She claims it helps her channel the
spirits of the saints and unlock the secrets of their suffering. The artist's daughter notes this channeling mainly
involves taking long breaks to read Sontag and chain-
smoking into a ceramic cross-shaped ashtray, but who
can say what strange guises the muses may take on?

Notice also, please, the plain plum carpeting, thin
in spots and worn through in others. The artist works
simply, as a penitent would, and does not insist on fancy
trappings in her humble working space. A straight-
backed wooden chair, some scissors and glue in a Dixie
cup, a cheap fiberboard table covered with sequins and
fabric scraps from Michael's, and tiny furniture from the
miniature store—this is all the artist requires to com-
plete her terrifying, ecstatic creations.

To your immediate right, our first exhibit: *The Torture of Saint Catherine.* You see here Catherine of Alexandria, the beautiful daughter of the king of Cyprus, in her prison cell being enthusiastically beaten with scorpions. Yes, well, those are actually tiny lobsters, not scorpions. It is *very* difficult to find scorpions in miniature, so you understand the artist must be inventive, flexible. That? White paint meant to read as dairy, since supposedly Catherine did not bleed red blood; her virginal veins spilled pure milk when she was tortured. The wheel? You see it outside the jail, waiting patiently for the martyr. The artist's daughter—assistant—enjoyed gluing the metal spikes to the cardboard very much.

Continuing our tour: on this old bookcase we see the artist's masterpiece, *The Eyes of Saint Lucy.* Lucy's eyes were torn from her sockets after she refused to relinquish her virginity (a common theme in medieval sainthood), and she carries them on a satin pillow. Yes, those are the candy known as silver bullets, for cookie decorating, but see how cleverly the irises are painted on! See the red stain on the white satin! See the jailer, still in his Dollhouse Dad brown polyester pants, cruelly laughing as our poor Lucy's soul prepares to spiral up to heaven! No great artwork arrives without suffering, and indeed for this particular piece the artist's house nearly burned down, when she left the oatmeal on the stove one morning while she scrubbed Lucy's yellow hair with Mane 'n Tail to take out stray incense ash. It was worth it, though; the artist identifies most with this particular piece and has long claimed Saint Lucy's power to see and unsee, heavenly vision a feast for her poor starved soul.

In the far corner, we can see what first appears to be a laser—red thread and wire—but is in fact the pain of Jesus on the cross, striking poor Saint Rita on the forehead with great violence. Fun fact: the artist's daughter had the stomach flu when her mother told her about the large suppurating wound Rita would receive from her injury, and how grateful she was for it, and the artist's daughter was never again able to eat properly in sight of uncovered injuries and sores.

Other dioramas you may walk about the room and observe: *The Penance of Saint Pelagia*, *The Stigmata of Siena's Catherine*, and another highlight, *Saint Agatha Having Her Breasts Hacked Off*. There are also several paintings on the wall for you to enjoy and reflect upon, including Saint Joan on her pyre and the poor toothless Saint Apollonia.

Please do not touch the exhibits; these figures are not for play, as the artist's children have been told time and time again. Nonetheless, we should admit an occasional saintly figure does make it outside to join in the holy wars of G.I. Joe and Barbie, or to serve as cannon fodder for the breaching of the Beamises' windows.

The artist completes approximately one diorama every two years, though she did take a yearlong hiatus after her only daughter was born.

WENDY BOUGHT THE POISON the day Hollis brought home the Feral Boy, though she didn't use it for a long time after. We called him Feral Boy, me and my brothers, because my father claimed he found him in a field out back of the auto parts factory, chasing buck naked after a corn snake. We thought that was the funniest thing we'd ever heard, and my brothers and I decided he must have been reared by wolves, like the boy in *The Jungle Book*. He was too little to know much or say much then, but my mother thought he looked an awful lot like Hollis and she said, all frost under her Virginia Slim, You expect me to raise that child?

Have a heart, said Hollis, and he held out his hands like a penitent. He'd come home from work early with the boy, so we knew it must be important. Hollis never left work early. His brown Buick coming up the drive, in need of a muffler, was a new sound this time of the afternoon, out of place and jarring as the *Jaws* theme. We all looked at the small boy clinging to my father's legs. He had long-ish hair that stuck up in places, but otherwise he was disappointingly normal. Shorts and sneakers and shirt like the rest of us, sullen glare and shins covered with scrapes.

He's not my brother, I said, and Wendy took my hand. Ours either, said my brothers, and they never stopped tormenting him after that, with pinches and punches and taunts and leaving-outs (the worst hurt of all).

He's not *anybody's* brother, said Hollis, tapping his watch nervously. He didn't look at Wendy. The boy's going to live with us, though, and we'll *treat* him like family. Wendy dropped my hand and went inside without a word. No one saw her for a long week, and when she emerged, ash-stained blouse and one eyebrow raised, she had painted something and then burned it in a coffee can. She never even told *me* what it was. Then, she bought the cyanide from a jeweler, and she kept it in her studio for ten years, though I didn't know about it until much later in the story.

Hollis promptly went back to work and started spending all his time there. He'd previously made it a point to be home by five, but now he stayed well into the evening hours. My brothers didn't treat Feral Boy like family, of course, but since they usually went off by themselves those days, first gold in the morning to last wan light at night in summer, I was stuck with Feral Boy. He was so very beautiful and shy. I had to protect him at school from the bullies and leeches, boys and girls both, and it was exhausting work. He was prickly and defensive, and often got quietly angry. He held long grudges over nothing at all, and he never made any real friends but me. I loved him, though, in the end, since he was soul-wild like me. We would go out into the fields behind the factory, or the wood next to the crick, and we would build forts and faery mounds. We would sacrifice field mice to the pagan gods and try to summon up demon servants. We would dance in the rain until we were soaking, trying to outshout the thunder.

We would pretend we were married and old, like Hollis and Wendy. Do you suppose I'll have affairs like

Hollis? he would ask. If you do, I told him, I'll kill you and bury you in the field where Hollis found you. That seemed to make him happy. FB never wanted any friends other than me, and I knew he was in love with me very early on. I knew I could be in love with him too, if I let myself, so I waited and put off deciding what to do about it until we were grown.

Wendy was forever trying to interest him in the saints, and she made him sit for a painting of John the Baptist once when we were in high school. You know, she told him, you were born of sin, like all men, and you must start atoning. Wendy had a way of being droll about the darkest sorts of things. It was never clear whether she was serious or not. She'd given up the Virginia Slims by then, but not the habit of speaking out of the corner of her mouth, and it gave her an odd air of ventriloquism. You might consider the priesthood, she said. Feral Boy, whom we called Michael sometimes at Wendy's baptismal insistence, was horrified at the suggestion.

I want to go to Hollywood, he said. I want to be a famous actor. He was certainly lovely enough, all dark hair and gold eyes and graceful lean limbs. It was just us by then; my brothers had fled the suburbs for school, or for other suburbs in other cities. Hollis had become president of the Western Auto Parts company, and he never really came home again after FB. That suited Wendy just fine. She was working on what she hoped would be her finest creation yet: *The Trial of Saint Joan*. The scale was to be massive, since she planned to use our old He-Man action figures for the judges, and Malibu Barbie for the Maid of Orleans.

HOLLIS AND HIS FAVORITE JOKES:
1. On disabilities. Q: Why did the one-handed man cross the road? A: To get to the second-hand shop.
2. On existentialism. Q: What do you call a person with no body and no nose? A: Nobody knows!
3. On horses. Q: Why did the bartender give the Clydesdale a drink of water? A: Because he was a little horse.
4. On parenting. Q: What did the buffalo say to his kid when he dropped him off? A: Bison.
5. On sacraments. Q: How do you make holy water? A: Boil the hell out of it.

DESPITE HER INITIAL REVULSION, Wendy grew more attached to FB than to my own brothers. They were so *male*, unsentimental and practical, uninterested in my mother's life or hobbies. They were equally indifferent to Hollis, and there was no pre-nostalgic sense they would be gone someday, because they already were. The elder talked of nothing but baseball, and the younger was a quiet blur; he couldn't stay still for a moment. They did just well enough in school to do fine, and they were popular and well-liked and played a sport each season. Wendy and Hollis never went to a game, but that didn't seem to bother my brothers at all. I played with them and tried hard to keep up, but when FB came along they receded, keeping their own counsel and circle. My mother was often angry at FB, who was dreamy to the point of exhaustion, but then again he was the only person on the planet who ever made Wendy smile. I didn't know she *could* smile until FB; we always figured her face just wasn't shaped that way. He could tumble about like a vaudeville actor, and sing like a sweet dazed dream, and his songs climbed up the smoke of Wendy's incense while we three plaited yarn hair for the doll heads of martyred Christians and their pagan persecutors.

———

READING COMPREHENSION:

1. Which of us did Wendy love most?
2. Why did Wendy often get angry at FB, and why did she call him Michael?
3. Where did my brothers fly to?
4. Why didn't my brothers take FB with them?
5. Should I have played a sport?
6. Should I have worked harder at making friends, less hard at protecting FB?
7. Was I sure, already, that it didn't matter; sure that somehow I would end up like Wendy,

shut in a smoke-filled room, worn beige carpets and doll limbs and lumps of putty heaped
on tables?

8. Was I sure, already, that my own wildness
would weird into Wendy's—a hidden dark,
full of shadows and blood and whispered
confessions? That I, too, would be held cap-
tive by the same men who claimed to love
my stray spirit?

Short Films for Feral Boy

Scene: Our sixth-grade classroom, where we wrote
each other notes on paper that smelled like Wendy's
incense and Hollis's cologne, coded to a frequency only
we two could understand.

Scene: Wendy's studio, where we tried to understand
about the martyrs through the cigarette smoke and the
paint and glue fumes, hazy with chemical feelings.

Scene: The parking lot of the local 7-Eleven, where
we sucked up Slurpees and smoked cigarettes bummed
from older kids and pretended to be panhandlers.

Scene: The swimming pool just down the road,
where we lay on white plastic lawn chairs, wrapped
in heat and sucking languidly on Pixy Stix and Dum
Dums, occasionally doing cannonballs off the diving
board into the deep end.

Scene: The scrubby field behind Hollis's factory, where we built a secret place on the windiest stump of a hill with sticks and rocks and leaves, and kissed each other silly because we were beautiful and bored.

Scene: My upstairs bedroom, where we lay pajama'd and chaste, side by side on my small ruffled bed, just like Tristan and Isolde.

Scene: The fancy party we snuck into, in the richer suburb next to ours. Where we crawled in through the open basement window, one of those old-fashioned ones with a crank and latch, and drank half a bottle of expensive scotch before they found us. Where we sat, in shame, on somebody's spotless white leather sofa, and watched the police car park in the driveway to take us back to Hollis and Wendy. Where Hollis said I shouldn't be running so free, and Wendy said it was your fault, and they both said they'd have to send you away, and I put my foot down in the middle of the new blue shag and said I'd follow you anywhere they sent you. The fight that followed, long and dreadful, when I said I loved you.

An Incomplete List of Saints Who Suffered from Stigmata

Saint Francis: wounds on feet, wrists, hands, and right side.

Saint Gemma: wounds and burning on hands, feet, and heart.

Saint Catherine of Siena: wounds on hands and feet, made invisible after prayers.

Saint Rita: a single thorn piercing her forehead, a sup-purating wound lasting forever.

Saint Hollis: gouges made on hands and feet—just after death, just before the police arrived to take his wife, my mother, into custody.

BECAUSE THERE IS NO GOD, my mother decided to play him, and the gods do love to watch the results of their own handiwork. My mother asked Hollis to stay home with her that day and, stunned, he drank his morning coffee and complied. Unfortunately for Hollis, he was the one-out-of-ten-people who can't smell potassium cyanide. Wendy could. The faint odor of bitter almonds hung about Hollis even after he'd drained his cup (quickly and efficiently as ever). She told me later she was unwilling to use a gun, given her first marriage and years spent on the roof of the range. And she was sure Hollis would approve at least the *efficiency* of a massive dose of cyanide, sure to slow and stop the respiratory system and the heart quickly. She wasn't prepared for the Prussian blue of his pop-eyed face, but as an artist she appreciated its aesthetic value.

The stigmata, as she explained to the police, were

merely sketches for a project she was working on. She saw the chance with a (near) live model and took it, though of course no blood was flowing through the body at that point. All the neighbors were outside on our perfectly manicured lawn, watching police put her in the patrol car, when FB and I came back home from school. She nodded toward us, her hair knotted over her skinny neck. She pushed her hands and eyes up heavenward. She's praying, said FB, but I shook my head. She was flying away, dissolving into wing and cloud and air and light. She was becoming her own miracle.

———

WE SPRINKLED BITS of Hollis over the Western Auto Parts Inc. branches in Muncie, Gary, Terre Haute, Elizabethtown, Hammond, and Bloomington. FB whispered under his breath during the service that Wendy's men seemed destined to become eternal punch lines, universal jokes. I told him that was because there was no god. Only wronged saints like Wendy.

My brothers came back for the ceremony, blamed me perfunctorily, and then dispersed again, bound for the real world. Wendy's lawyer got her into a nice minimum-security mental institution, and I visit her there every third Thursday of the month. She's allowed paints and paper and is still working on a massive mural of her favorite, Saint Joan. Wendy says now that she has first-hand experience of a trial she feels ready for such an undertaking. She likes the simplicity, the enforced quiet and structure of her small bare days. FB visits with me whenever he's home from Hollywood, which is less and less often these days. He is very busy working, and the gossip magazines tie him to all manner of glamorous ladies, but I know the truth: we swore never to love another as long as we're both alive. We can't be lovers—Wendy told us why—but we'll be together in our shared loneliness. It's a good vow, almost as holy as a religion.

I spend my days in the fields behind the house, missing FB and Wendy, picking wildflowers. At dusk I bring them home to Wendy's studio—my studio—and I get to work. I'm making a diorama of Saint Urith of Chittlehampton; her stepmother had her killed by harvesters with scythes. The flowers line the spots where her blood soaked the earth. Legend says that red gave way to white, to great blooms of yellow, of green and pink and palest blue; legend says spring itself was born of Urith's suffering. Life blossoming out of the long dark stain of winter.

We Were a Storybook
Back Then

———————————◆━━➤

EVERYBODY KNEW ABOUT OLIVER. SOMETIMES SHE WOULD leave the house in her sister's ballet costumes, pink tutus and pearl-colored sequins. It was easy to believe that she was a princess; she was fair and pretty and hazed through the world like soft smoke. She wasn't anything like the rest of us—she didn't like video games or flag football or frogs or fireworks. Oliver would steal our mothers' scarves and put on shows for us, hand-lettered signs sprinkled with glitter announcing her Dance of the Seven Veils. Our G.I. Joes and Barbies sat on the grass in silence, enchanted troops at a USO show. We made a small kingdom for ourselves.

The thing about Oliver: she was under a spell. She was really the princess of a far-off land but her father the king had remarried, and her wicked and terrible step-mother had turned her into a small boy out of jealousy. And then this wicked stepmother cast her out for good. She was exiled to the suburbs of Omaha, Nebraska.

Of course we believed it was a spell. It was easier to understand than the grunts and eye-rolls our fathers made when they saw Oliver, when we mentioned Oliver, when the thought of Oliver crossed their minds. Our big, bearded fathers seemed afraid, though we didn't understand how they could be afraid of anything.

All through childhood, through birthday parties and recesses and snowball fights and school dances, we tried to help Oliver break the spell. We tried spitting in the holy water, we played our Monkees records backwards, we consulted the Ouija board and tarot cards and Carly Manley's psychic aunt. We even tried hypnosis, *chanting light as a feather, stiff as a board*, while Oliver lay awake and sighing in satin. We expected to break the spell soon; all that was needed was a certain flower, a certain word, a certain gesture performed on a moonlit night while humming a certain tune. We read fairy tales to find clues. We waited for Oliver's fairy godmother to show up, wise and plump. We waited for the king to ride to Omaha with his royal retinue, seeking his cursed daughter. We waited up many midnights to watch the illusion dissolve, Cinderella in reverse. We waited for glass slippers to appear.

Oliver's family moved away from the neighborhood just as we were struck with our own terrible curse: puberty. We were too self-absorbed to say goodbye. We were sad, though, because Oliver was our only link to something beautiful, a strange sort of magic that was otherwise lost to us.

Rabbit by Rabbit

———————————⦁➤

THE GIRL IS DRINKING RED WINE IN THE NURSERY. SHE IS pregnant. She is languid; she is huge and hazy and full of vague hopes for the future. She is populating a doll-house for her child, figure by figure, family member by family member. The house is a painstaking replica of her own, built by her husband before he marched off to battle. The dolls are her dreams, each room a tableau of future children and future wishes. None of which will exactly come true. The father of this baby has just been shot for desertion, and will not return from this war or any other. She will go into labor with her hands round the letter, ink smeared in soft smudges over her swollen palms.

Many years later she will ask her grandchildren, Was that one or two wars ago? A husband or several? She will be possessed, by then, of the magic of forgetting. Rabbit by rabbit, the past will go into the hat.

In will go husbands, children, lovers, friends, streetcars, swimming, low-heeled shoes, high-necked dresses, strawberry pies, fortune-tellers at the fair, hay bales and harpsichords and half-baked schemes she dreamt up when she was a little girl. In will go lamps and door-stops and baking bread and chimneys and pipe smoke and paintings and symphonies and stars. In will go all the words for these things, or most of them, anyway. By the time she meets her first great-great-granddaughter, she will not even remember the word for love. But she will still have the dollhouse, worn through and tumbled, dolls with no faces and walls dark with handprints. She will spend the most of her time with it, moving room to room as if she were a doll, forehead pressed against the clouded glass windows. She will wait and dream instructions from the dolls inside. She will wonder at their threadbare clothes and understand the memory of love collects here somehow.

Rabbit by rabbit, into the hat: pictures, people, machines—all will accelerate and eventually pursue one another with frantic, herky-jerky stop-starts, flickering in and out of range. Start in sepia tones, progress to perfect Technicolor saturation.

Next, the memory of traumas; self and the world's. Everything that burns: grass, forests, skin, aircraft, cities, crops. Her second husband to smoke. Her two sons to fever. Her daughter: a strange cult and a series of feverish marriages and too many children she didn't quite love. Maps, too, gone, so no path can be left to trace through the wreckage.

The good young life: spent tan, spent cycling, spent golfing—tennis lessons at Biarritz from the nice young pro with the pet spiders. A neck, long and swanlike. Her admirers, astonished, a beige blur behind the sudden brilliance of her boyfriend. He, the soldier in scarlet. She the grieving widow, beautiful and child-laden, the Madonna in black brocade.

Then childbirth, always a swollen breast, always a husband somewhere off in the middle distance with a paper and a pipe. A lake house, a black lace dress. Then he her favorite husband. He'll teach her to shoot, to jump nude into a fountain and swim in jazz, to fly from a window, fly into a needle, to squander, squander, squander joy until you've used up all your teeth and hair and laughter. All flown, all gone, all stuffed like colorful crepe streamers into the magic hat.

After, the world gone gray at first, then faded to silver, still mechanical in its new and dreamless age. Her first glimpse of the Great Structures; she'll shimmy up in denim overalls and stand at the vanishing point. She'll pity the world below, pointillistic, vague and undefined. Into the hat, the flying machines.

To be dissolved: the long nights, alone in dark clubs and alone in dark bars and alone in dark bedrooms, trying desperately to find light.

To be dissolved: the visits from grandchildren, hesitant and shy. The smell of young skin, too much memory in that downy scent. But always enough love, always hands in the dollhouse, more figures always needed.

Finally tragedy, finally weeping. Finally the memory of man's hubris. Finally the iceberg, the bomb, the burn always lurking to fill the trenches, the beaches, the ovens, the jungles, the deserts. The hubris that will eat up trees and children and even the dead with relish; the way man will peel history like an onion, or sometimes drill a hole right through.

The men. The last to go: the men, the collective men, and she will finally do the leaving for once. She's held to them too long, given them too much place of importance in her own long life history. No more.

She will press her old frame to the rotting roof of the dollhouse, finally emptied, hollow and ready to enter. Her own old face will be nearly gone, a smear of red for lips, two smears of bleary blue for eyes. Her clothes will be simple and coarse, her head a wooden O. She'll push and push through until those long-ago rooms are hers again; until she finds a new set of stages for a new set of lives. She'll push until she finds herself in a child's palm, a new small vessel for someone else's dreams.

But now, in this moment, she puts down her wine. She lowers her huge, tired frame to the floor and smiles, puts her hand on her belly and imagines the strange small vessel inside. She tells herself: Remember this. Remember it all.

Through the Looking-Glass

———————◆———

I T WAS THE EMPTY JIM BEAM BOTTLE ON ITS SIDE IN THE SUL-
len yellow shower, the fluorescent sign flickering on
the roof, the bedsprings creaking in the room next door.

It was the stained beige carpet and way he shouted
when he came in.

It was the way she lay for hours, facedown on that
carpet, trussed and always with the camera at her back.
It was the way the room was sometimes green, was
sometimes gray, was sometimes a cheap room-to-let
and sometimes a cheap roadside motel and sometimes a
cheap county jail cell—but always cheap, always faded
and frayed as the wallpaper that sometimes lined these
walls. It was the way the men in suits filed in, talking
on their handsets or their earpieces and taking notes
and casting eyes back and forth, fishing for visions in the
close and clammy air.

It was the way she sometimes perched at the vanity,

watched him enter as a tall swift triptych through the mir-
rors, or as a prisoner, battered. It was the way she combed
her hair, the way she put on lipstick, the way she dragged
mascara through her lashes while she listened to the clock
tick on and on. It was the way he said he liked her better
without makeup. It was the way he held her throat, the
way she didn't scream, the way he called her Alice though
that was not her name, had never been her name. It was
the way they both signed the ledger, also not their real
names, checking in and out each day, heading home sep-
arately, he in his car, she in worn tennis shoes, walking
three miles to the bus to her apartment where she washed
her face, her arms, her legs, her feet and toes, her stomach.

It was the way she sometimes left him tied up in the
bathtub for hours, inches of water wrinkling his thin
white skin, casting him in old man's costume. The way
his arms and legs grew thatched and scarred as train
tracks, the way she always found fresh flesh to cut. The
way the men in suits would take pictures, bending down,
frowning at the carpet like crime scene photographers.
The way her clothes were always crumpled on that carpet. The way she sometimes wore layers of clothes, the
way sometimes there were never enough clothes, the way
sometimes there was never enough fabric in the world to
cover her over and swallow her under.

The way they avoided eye contact but every now and
then their gazes would join, would lock, would jolt them
apart, the third rail of desire. The way they would sometimes forget to scratch or scream or scrape or otherwise

draw blood and would instead hold each other, skin and breath and damaged heart, until they fell asleep in that vibrating bed. The way they would sometimes turn off the recording devices and stash the cat-o'-nine-tails and the cattle prod and hide the handcuffs in the drawer next to the King James Bible. The way they would sometimes dress one another, he in a tux and she in a gown, the way they would bow to one another, the way they would sip champagne and smile politely over their prime rib. The way he would mention moonlight on the Seine. The way she would shiver.

The way they would finally say I love you and I love you too and the way alarms would shriek and the way the men in suits would invade in an army of red ties and bulletproof vests. The way the room would shrink and blacken the way the room would dim the way the blood would pool and churn in the bath the way their names their real names would finally echo soft but true in tune like nothing else in this cruel circus called the world when they finally shut off the lights.

The Noises from the Neighbors Upstairs:
A Nightly Log

Night One

The noises are small, faint scratches and scrapes. We lie in bed and look at the ceiling, drowsy, unconcerned. Rats in the walls, you say. Maybe a squirrel.

I think it's the ceiling, not the walls. But I defer to you at night, because never in any way am I getting out of bed and investigating things.

Night Two

The noises are a little louder, scuffles and thumps, like someone moving furniture. Christ's sake, I say. Are they moving or what?

Who moves out at midnight, you say, but come on, plenty of our neighbors have. Remember the couple across the hall? You went out shirtless and bellowing, and scared the shit out of a perfectly nice pair of newlyweds.

Hopefully they'll be out soon, I say. I fall asleep half-listening for the outside door to slam shut.

Night Three

I'm up late tonight, on deadline. It's a profile of a celebrity I hate, but I need the money, and so I'm already pissed and ready to fight when the bowling ball falls overhead.

At least that's what it sounds like, a fucking bowling ball, dropped from a great height in the apartment. I grab a broom and I jab at the ceiling. Three times, with *intention*. What the fuck, I yell. The neighbor next door yells back and pounds on my wall. Shut up, he says, barely muffled by the paper-thin barrier. He throws loud parties every other weekend, smokers on the balcony till 3 a.m., shitty country music, he should talk. Another bowling ball slams, and I instinctively cover my head. Can the floors take this? I have no idea how my apartment is built. Every fix is half-assed, every surface slathered with too much white paint. The floors could be rot underneath, for all I know.

You emerge from our bedroom. You have your emoji underwear on and also nothing else. I pray to the patron saint of people scarred by nudity that you don't start up the stairs in a fury, not before I can stop you. What the FUCK, you say.

I KNOW, I say. That's what I said. What the fuck.

A third bowling ball drops. A dog barks. I fling myself onto the couch. I'll tell building management tomorrow, you say, and I breathe a sigh of minor relief. We don't get much sleep.

Night Four

I am hitting you on the shoulder, Wake up, wake up. Does our neighbor have dogs, I ask.

No dogs allowed, you say, sleepy and annoyed. You can't have dogs in the building, you know that.

I do know that. We wanted a dog, a little one, but your sister got kicked out of her building when that dumb Chow Chow barked all the time, and we can't afford an eviction. Not right now. We can barely afford pizza. So do you hear that growling?

You listen. You frown. Yeah, you say. I do. What is that? It sounds like . . . a bear or something. It sounds *big*.

We lie in bed and joke for a while about what the neighbors might be doing upstairs. Running a canine bowling alley? Smuggling Russian bears to American circuses? Darker thoughts, too—a dog meat supplier?

What if it's human trafficking, you ask. It happens everywhere, you know. We both lie still for a moment, frowning, worried, possibly complicit. Then we laugh.

Oh for fuck's sake, I say.

Night Five

You wake me this time, and your hand is over my mouth. I smell toothpaste. My heart flops over. Shhhh, you say. Listen.

I can hear it right away—crying. Someone is crying

upstairs, a woman or a child. Or is it a dog, whimpering? Oh my god, I say. What should we do? We made all those jokes. We laughed! What if somebody's really in trouble up there?

Before you can answer, there's a new sound—a snarl, and another sound like a crunch. Teeth in bone.

Shit, you say. You sit up fast. I'm still lying there, chin under the covers even though it's hot tonight. I still believe in under the covers.

It might just be a *really* big dog. Eating a raw chicken. Or a wolf? Maybe they have a wolf. SLAM. SLAM. SLAM. Now it's like a basketball, now like ten basketballs, now it's like it's raining basketballs up there. Basketball hailstorm, with a chance of—there it is—bowling balls. Crunch. Slam. Smash. Why isn't the whole apartment awake?

Then silence. Serious silence, the eye of the nightmare.

And then, a growl, like nothing I've ever heard in my life, weird and raspy, and a scream. A scream, I swear it. Then the crying again, soft but insistent, like rain on skin.

That's fucking it, you say. I'm going upstairs. It's obviously some kind of fucking joke, or a loud movie, or something. It has to stop.

No! I sit up, clutch your arm. You can't! What if there really is some kind of animal up there?

I'm just going to knock on the door, you say. Animals can't open doors.

Werewolves can, I say. I don't know if this is strictly

true, and wouldn't claws get in the way, probably, and obviously it depends on whether it's a more or less anthropomorphic werewolf, but there's no doubt I suddenly *believe* in werewolves.

And ghosts. And poltergeists. And vampires. And haunted houses. And murderous neighbors running illicit animal meat farms. Don't go, I say.

But you are pulling on your jeans, you are tying your shoes, you are grabbing your keys, you are opening the door. Take your phone! I shout. You are rolling your eyes, you are gone.

I listen to your footsteps fading down the hall. I listen to them coming back, one floor up. I listen to the knocking, loud, persistent, then stopping. I wait for a scream. I wait for a shout. I wait for the muted tone of polite conversation. I wait for anything other than this silence, dark and thick as smoke. I hold my breath against it and I wait, and I wait, and I wait.

Our Geographic History

―――――――――――――→

DEARBORN, MICHIGAN: HERE IS WHERE I TOLD YOU NOT TO buy that fucking 7-Eleven franchise. You couldn't even remember to pick up the kid from the sitter, so how were you going to keep track of how many Hot Pockets to buy and whether or not the hot dogs had been cooking for days or weeks? How much green shit to put in the Slurpee machine?

Existential Suffering, USA: Here is where I understand our complaints have been vague. I understand it is offputting to you, to your obsession with a certain certainty.

Fort Wayne, Indiana: Here is where I used to think you had given your whole body to Jesus Christ, all those delicious lusts and longings. I used to admire your purity, so unsullied that you could not even touch a breast or kiss a mouth.

Columbia City, Indiana: Here is where I read them all, book after book in the Columbia City Central Library. Here is where I learned about myths and maps. Here is where I traced my pink-sparkled fingernail over the lines that my parents traveled, over the landscape of the past. Here is where I learned what vagrants we are, we whose people were farmers once. Tied to the land for years, we were pushed out, exiled as Ahasuerus.

Here, too, is where I dreamed of futures: all those unspoiled dots, waiting to expand into towns, into cities, into grand tall buildings and crowds of people all waiting for something to happen. Here, too, is where I dreamed of the moon: round and open and waiting to give us everything we needed.

Dead center of my heart: Here is where you lived for a long time, before the kid was born, before you started drinking all day. Here is where you lived while I think we loved each other. At least, I loved you enough to feed us both for a while, enough to paper over the spreading damage. Here is where you kissed me and gave me a ring, and I believed in that diamond like I believed in

fairy tales. Even though I was old enough to know nei-
ther was real.

Dearborn, Michigan: Here is where the milk went sour.
And here is where the kids stole cigarettes when you
were pumping gas. And here is where Ahmed got shot
on the overnight shift, survived thank god or whoever.
I got the call when you were dead drunk. I dropped the
kid off at Mrs. Tiffany's, called in sick to the pharmacy,
and then I drove to St. Joe's. They had Ahmed in a room,
IV and all, but he said he was okay. I told him not to go
back and he said he wouldn't, said his brother owns a
place, they do coffee and donuts, said he'd go work for
him. Ahmed was so happy, more happy than I'd ever
see him—usually he's just like, Here's your change and
That'll be sixteen twenty-five. The nurse came in and
said visiting time was up now, and Ahmed reached out
for my hand and patted it, like he was comforting me. It's
a new start, he said.

The muffled quiet of the womb: Here is where we got our
new starts, our very first starts.

Huntersville, Indiana: Here is where I met you after my
family moved, where I went to your youth group because
I thought you looked like what Kurt Cobain might look

like if he was a born-again. I sat on the carpet while everybody prayed, holding one hand up like they needed to ask god a question. Then everyone looked at me, and I didn't say anything but inside I was like, Oh, fuck, no. But then you smiled at me, and I felt it then, that good feeling, and you nodded, like, Go on, and so I said Okay, Jesus can come into my life I guess. It made all those people so happy, and it made you happier, so I suppose it was a small thing. And you felt okay about loving me then.

Lansing, Michigan: Here is where we ended up, after the franchise went bust. You came home last Christmas, drank a case of Coors, and passed out in front of the tree. I had to haul your ass to the bedroom by myself because the kid was only three, and what was that going to do, her seeing you unconscious, all those crushed cans and tinsel and you under the soft red and white lights. You slept it off the next morning while the kid and I opened our gifts and then we left for good.

Underneath the sky somewhere between Michigan and Indiana and you: Here is the moon, that same shape I've been looking at since I was small and thought I might do bigger things. Now I'm the deserted bride howling up against it. It's bigger and emptier than me. It's something to hold my sorrows, I suppose. It's something for you to remember me by.

DEATH DESERVES ALL CAPS:
On Planning for
My (Very Far-Off) Funeral

1. Get it right, or I will haunt you all.
2. I write "far-off" so my parents, who find me morbid, will think of wills and distant relations instead
   of smashed china and the unreliability of actuarial
   science. "Very" was added to preserve the rhythmic
   integrity of the line. The parenthesis was included
   to please my fiancé—Hello, A.—who is an annoying stickler for punctuation. He is also an annoying
   stickler for Not Eating in Bed, and for Telling Others
   When They Are Wrong on a Small Point. He may or
   may not be invited to the final celebration.
3. Seriously, you have a lot of time to plan this thing. I
   don't intend on heading into the metaphysical sun-
   set for quite some time.
4. But still, who doesn't think about death, every
   moment of every day? I simply don't see how one
   could exist otherwise, in such earthly limbo, excuse

the intentional misuse of the word. Mrs. Peters in the seventh grade accused me of being a goth and my dear parents (Dear Mother and *Dearest* Stepfather, I'll probably have forgiven you by the time I'm dead, perhaps) sent me to the Catholic girls' school in Kent to retrain me, and really, is there anything more inclined to train someone to think exclusively of death—manner and method of, and What Lies Beyond—than a *Catholic school education*?

5. I'm excited to be a ghost and that's the truth. I don't fear the banality of endless earthly hauntings, stalking you all through the emotional landscapes of Whole Foods and holidays. No, no, it's the celestial idea of the afterlife I fear, living in the stars or clouds or rain or something—like being on a never-ending plane ride where there isn't any Xanax and everyone keeps talking about the most obscure Greek gods and you feel so left out and so untethered.

6. To be clear, I don't want a funeral. I want a memorial service, a sort of celebration or party. The term "funeral" is only used as a generic marker, a shared cultural symbol to let others know that: (1) I am dead and (2) hope is the thing with feathers, and I have always been allergic to down.

7. Seriously, no funeral. No bodies, no Bibles, no biographies. No sermon or studied sad faces. Just my life strung out in beautiful films projected on the sides of buildings and the understanding that you are all the poorer for the passing of it.

8. Rending of garments is acceptable, though unlikely to succeed, modern fabrics being what they are.

9. Dreams are boring: please don't share yours.

10. No pictures age 9–16. See item 1. No Instagramming or live tweeting my death. See item 1.

11. I would be pleased with a brief, bright ceremony held in front of *The Physical Impossibility of Death in the Mind of Someone Living*, but I know we are all supposed to disapprove of Damien Hirst now. So I suppose I should settle for the sea, which is really the same thing.

12. Stop talking about death, people always say. As if it were taboo. As if it weren't the Great Leveler. I was trained up to a life of accountancy and account-settling, so how can I not include it in my calculations? WHO DOESN'T LIE AWAKE AT NIGHT AND THINK ABOUT DEATH? I don't believe it. Death deserves all caps. To deny it is like denying that you eat sandwiches. Everyone eats death. My last girlfriend broke up with me because she had a death allergy. So she said. She also wore a Hello Kitty anklet everywhere, even in the shower, because it was supposedly lucky, and how magical thinking isn't about death I'm not quite sure but Hello, E., I certainly hope no one invites you to this death celebration. We met as accountants who hated our jobs but I suspect now that you were just pretending and I've always hated pretenders even more. Anyhow at my celebration you'd probably stand there with your

banker wife (and her inappropriate Crocs like that bitch couldn't afford some decent shoes) and try to read Ayn Rand to the assembly.

13. Related: anyone who reads Ayn Rand, or attempts to read Ayn Rand, will be forcibly ejected from the proceedings.

14. If anyone plays or sings "Candle in the Wind," I will extra haunt them.

15. Is it possible to make of me into a kind of champagne? Or better yet, whiskey—bury me in a peaty bog and get everybody good and drunk on me? I always wanted to be a bartender, but the parents warned me about my Uncle Ed too often. I was trained up to make money, not to drink it. Before my favorite brother, D., died, before in fact he graduated to fentanyl and vodka cocktails, he used to love scotch so much it was a family joke. Because we're Irish! Haha, ha, haha. Addiction, it runs in our family and this funeral—I mean celebration—will certainly be no place to deny that. Hard truth will be spoken, indulgences indulged. I can't wait to see D. in the afterlife, so there had better be an afterlife. And he better be clean in it. I really miss him.

16. I'm paying, so everyone crowd in! The neighbors, my stylist, my therapist, the panhandlers. All the animals from the zoo. The more the merrier. The more the more memorial. The immemorial, scattered through skies of memory in a thousand probably off-base but well-meant memories of me.

17. Yes, there will be proceedings. Possibly elephants. Certainly tigers. Probably not bears, as they are unpredictable and entirely too Russian for what will on the whole be a pretty Midwestern affair.

18. Probably someone should read Sir Thomas Browne. I wish that the entire body of Shakespeare's work wasn't so *done*. I mean, someone could read something from *Coriolanus*, but that seems to defeat the purpose of demanding superlatives. Do I need my funeral to be *different*, to be unique? Are we worried about this sort of thing past the point where the heart collapses and the lungs fill with larvae? I wish that Kissinger hadn't wasted "I shall not look upon his like again" on Nixon. Though I suppose if it was read at my funeral it would confuse literal-minded attendees. They might suspect they had come to the wrong service. My easily shocked conservative family has always been concerned about my fidelity to gender. After a succession of girlfriends, the family was audibly relieved when I found a man. I could have married an escaped convict and still they'd have celebrated my return to the fold. As a ghost perhaps I'll come back as a man, especially to haunt them. Or perhaps ghosts have no gender. A comforting thought. In the meantime, A. and I will surely share a succession of mistresses, younger and plumper as the years go by.

19. Every funeral must be cliché. In the end there are so many deaths, and only a handful of geniuses to hold the glass up to them. This is not a funeral, no. But it

will still be a cliché. A.'s and my children will weep, and someone will clutch at a handkerchief, and someone else will wear entirely too much black to be sincere. My two sisters or my other brother might attend, if their grandchildren don't have any soccer tournaments that day and they don't mind the traffic on the drive into the city. If I've accomplished anything in my life by then, big *if*, then someone important may speak about it. Now husband A. will look distinguished and sad, if he's still around, and I'm sure that bastard (Hi darling) will be such an annoyingly handsome old man that someone younger will fall in love with him then and there and he'll mourn me all of five minutes. I hope our children stop speaking to him after that.

20. I'm not sure how much dancing I want. Definitely no DJ. A nice jazz quartet might be tasteful, I suppose. Classical music would be too on the nose. On the other hand, perhaps we'll need a good band. I have some sexy exes I would dearly love to dance with again, even and especially as a ghost.

21. Would it be a disaster if the memorial *wasn't* tasteful? Shouldn't death, the great renewal, be a sort of breathless bacchanalia, anyhow? Shouldn't I choose the whirling of dervishes over the starched collars and dusty mourning of the barely bored and the mentally absent? Perhaps my family would learn to love one another at my celebration. Perhaps they'd drop repression for a moment, just one, and stop

slicing into one another for the sake of respectability. Perhaps pigs will grow wings, as they say, and the halls of hell will empty and grow cold.

22. Could we pretend death is really a sort of starting over? Or is that just too much to ask? Could we refrain from imagining one another in our underclothes, in our skin, in our bones, in our foaming muscle and softening fat to feed and fortify the loamy soil we float in? Could we refrain from the cranking of hymns, from the showing of slideshows, from the off-center programs made in Microsoft Word over our lunch breaks, littered with lachrymose sentiment and wrong-aspect-ratio pictures where we look, ashamed, at the camera—suddenly so embarrassed to be alive? Standing in front of the Taj Mahal, or in Times Square, in places teeming with life while we stop what isn't ours to stop and claim it like a big-game hunter in the Nairobi, while we nail down our trophies of space and seize this pretense, this rarified air that we pretend is ours alone? While we understand that we are all just falling through, like Alice down the rabbit hole, and taking snapshots on the way of all the wrong-sized things and places we may find ourselves, oh funny man-shaped spaces, because what else, really, can we be expected to do with this tiny vial of time on earth?

23. No shorts, or cold-shoulder dresses. And for god's sake, no poetry.

A Wholly New and Novel Act, with Monsters

I N LATE 1956, THE CLASSIC CIRCUS DIED AND SO DID SUSAN Malone, the world's youngest lion tamer. At six she had been known as the Laughing Maid, for taunting the lions, leaping lightly out of the way of their subsequent rage. At ten, she'd retired to Pensacola and taken possession of the defunct King Circus's auctioned-off lions. She was bitten in the thigh and arm before being dragged off into the bushes and eaten for breakfast.

In early days, "circus" described a wide variety of attractions, from a simple caged animal to a tent with featured aquatic acts, aerialists, equestrians, clowns, and bicycle races. There were bands and ballets and even sea battles fought in wide, water-filled arenas. The beasts languished in cages, more portable zoos than animal acts. Joseph Handler's eighteenth-century show, "A Wholly New and Novel Act, with Monsters as Seen in their Natural Environs, TERRIFYING AND SHOCKING," was in fact

151

just a small, barred wagon crowded with malnourished leopards illegally smuggled in from Madagascar.

Then Isaac A. Van Amburgh stuck his arm and head into a cage of lions in 1862. And the crowd, as they say, went wild.

Famous Ringling Bros. lion tamer Daniel Descartes died in 1892 after his arm was torn off, exactly ten years to the day after his brother was killed. Both were mauled by the lions they worked with, in what observers said were unprovoked attacks. Three other family members were hurt or killed by the family business in the intervening years. One cousin told his local paper it was the price one paid to make bargains with the wild. Animals rarely honor such bargains, and humans even less often. He had chosen to open a butcher shop instead.

Elephants and bears were introduced to circuses well after the big cats, to significantly more fanfare. They were also more dangerous, their attacks more sensational. Some claimed, of course, that this was the whole point. Revenge as a story, attack as an art form. A wholly new and novel act.

In all instances, the animals' revenge was short-lived. Topsy was, of course, electrocuted, and Mary hung from a crane. Dino and Barry were shot, Marvin poisoned, the King Circus lions all quietly sold for their meat and bones. In some cases the executions were public and publicized; in some cases the deaths were kept quiet. In a few cases the animals were allowed to live—not because trainers were softhearted, but owners were thrifty and refused to buy new animals. In all cases the animals were eventually pronounced "destroyed," and in all cases they probably were.

Thomas Macarte, known as Massarti, was scalped and torn apart by four lions in front of a full house. Children suffered nightmares so severe they said they carried them in the blood, like a disease. Their descendants claim they still dream of dreadful sounds and empty rings, blood spattered over the sawdust-covered floors.

When the Husband Grew Wings

THE WIFE THOUGHT THE HUSBAND LACKED SPIRIT. HE WOULD
hunch silent over his breakfast in the mornings,
hands pale and cold as his cereal, his hair the color of
cubicles. They married because the wife thought she
could open him up, pull out wild Irish weather. But
when she tried she found a map of Cleveland instead. Her
days grew long and endless as parades.

So one day the wife sprinkled a little powder over the
husband's cornflakes. It was a special power, meant to
make things grow, like spirits, yes, but sometimes eye-
balls or teeth or toenails. You could never tell with this
particular substance, so the wife crossed her fingers as
the husband slurped up the powder. Then the husband
slumped and fell out of his chair, and as he lay there on
the floor, the wife took his pulse. It was sometimes hard
to tell if the husband was dead or just lifeless. As she
pressed her fingers to his wrist, the wife noticed a faint

yellowish smoke hanging over the husband's back in the vague shape of wings. A pair of wings. Aha, she said.

It took a week for the wings to solidify. Meanwhile, the husband hardly seemed to notice them. He made room for them when he sat, true, and at night he started sleeping on his side, but he never said a word about his wings. They mostly stayed folded, a long soft lump under his suit jacket. The wife asked him once if his coworkers noticed anything different about him. He looked at her neck and shrugged, and she couldn't tell if the shrug meant no or yes or what's to notice, so she didn't ask again. She waited to see if he would fly. She started finding excuses to spend time outside, taped pictures of birds and planes in flight to the refrigerator door. She talked about taking up stargazing. But nothing happened. The husband seemed to have no interest at all in his brand-new wings.

One night at dinner, tired of wondering, she asked if he had flown. His weak, wandering eyes grazed her chin, confused. No, he finally said. I haven't tried. Should I? She nodded, exasperated but eager, and watched as he carefully unbuttoned his shirt, lifted his undershirt over his head, arched his back and let his wings slowly unfold. He looked surprised as the feathers fluttered, air currents stirred, but he lifted himself above the kitchen tile. He went up until he bumped against the plaster ceiling. Then he drifted back down to the ground, somewhat awkwardly. He folded the wings away, put on his undershirt and shirt again, and sat down. He picked up his fork. He frowned.

I really can't see the point, he said.

Of what, asked the wife.

Of wings, said the husband.

So the next morning, she sprinkled a little powder over her own cornflakes. It didn't hurt much—a little pulling and aching, like teeth coming in. After the husband went to work, she took off her shirt and stared. The wings were cream-colored, shot through with lilac and soft brown. She marveled at their loveliness, and how easily they moved with her, how gracefully they spanned her shoulder blades. She flexed them, tested them, felt the wind move through them powerful as engines.

And then, she flew away.

The Language of the Stars

-------------◆------

Celestial Time

The future, it turns out, looks a lot like the nineties. Do you remember those old television programs, the ones highlighting D-list celebrities, fashion mistakes? Cataloging fads like fades? Neons and novelty songs and 2-D video games?

This is a future bereft of all such bright trappings. Think instead clumsy car phones, gray pleated pants, office parks and corporate-ladder climbing. Think overtime and pagers. Think shared custody. Think children's breakfast cereal, eaten alone, in the dark.

But I still have you, Emmaline. I still love you, I still summon you, I call you up, the vision of the way you were. The way the summer sun could make a story of your copper skin and hair. The way your freckles faded in the winter and your eyes looked tired and kinder. The way you laughed, more generous than you really were, and far too loud.

Do you still laugh, Emmaline? Do you ever miss the sun?

Aberration

We have no idea what we look like to the robots. We know exactly what the robots ought to look like; or at least, we know what they looked like when we built them. They looked like us. They still *appear* to look like us.

But now, like so many things, we assume they have no fixed form. We assume they have evolved beyond shape. We suspect they sometimes step inside our skins; that sometimes, unbodied, they open our lives like envelopes, peer inside, fold in new dreams.

We have no idea if the robots have developed a language of their own. They are so inscrutable, so distant and cold, so like the stars in their singular orbits. What language do the stars speak?

Spectral Features

Each day, we settle into narrow cubicles, open paper calendars, mark important dates in red ink. We glance at framed school pictures of the children we don't see for more than a few moments each night, once they are sound asleep. We hold endless meetings in conference rooms, hold lengthy and serious phone conversations over big black plastic receivers. We put people on indefinite hold.

Our work, of course, does not exist; rather, it is a nagging suggestion, a vapor trail, a troubled miasma that surrounds us and sticks with a strange insistence. It worries us always.

Our future was more hopeful once. Not this aimless purposefulness, these itineraries full of meetings about meetings. The robots gave us leisure, at first. Blue water, white sand, clean city sidewalks. Time to linger, to putter. To frequent coffee shops and concerts and bars, to linger longer in restaurants. To catch up with old friends. Time, at last, with children, with spouses, with aging parents and grandparents.

We think it was that last gift that did us in. No one wants to spend that much time with the people they love. We gave up the ghost, and though I think the robots were baffled, they gave us ghost lives in return. Phantom productivity. Days full of so much serious nothing. The robots, so mathematically pure, provide addition only, or subtraction only. There is nothing in between.

It is rumored that there is another sort of space, a separate place for those with different dreams. Mind-altering substances, strange sex, darker fantasies. It may be this is why our offices feel so strangely deserted. Sometimes it seems I can go weeks without encountering another human, though the HR bot is very warm and chatty. She asks about you, Emmaline, every now and then.

Abluvion

They don't understand, the robots, how our memories eroded. They don't understand how memories are just runoff, washed away in the end like everything else.

We cannot know exactly what the robots intended—the robots, like angels, are ineffable—but I believe they also meant for us to keep the past. Powerful processors, they could never have understood how fast the human memory fades. Not in eons, or even generations, but in decades, years, days. If they feel pity, the robots must surely pity us for this.

Or perhaps they envy us? There is pain in memory, after all. I've heard of a rare disease humans had, once, where no memory could be shed, not even the slightest errand, nose twitch, conversation. How terrible that must have been, never to lose the most acute embarrassment and suffering, always to keep thumbing through minutiae just to find the things that actually mattered. So perhaps I am wrong, and it is the robots draining our memory banks. Perhaps they are sparing us suffering, the burden of the chronicler theirs alone.

Interstellar Abundances

Oh, Emmaline, Emmaline, I would have jumped off a mountain for you, back on Earth. I would have drowned myself, shot myself, baked myself in a pie for you. I would have kept myself to myself if you'd loved me. I wouldn't have texted you, not after ten.

The robots have said that I alone am stubborn. Kind and terrible in their patience, they have gently told me I still carry my past with me.

Why, the robots ask, must you remake your old worlds, cling so tightly to your old same sadness? Even in our sky ships, you dream of things we don't understand: castles, passion, love. Dragons?

It's all for you, of course. I have not given up my passion for you. I bind you, like the knights of old, my honor in a silk scarf I stole from your desk. It is tied to my sleeve. It is made of scent and stars. It has grown, it's true, a little bit musty. Like most things.

I remember that night when you stood under all those stars, when there were still selfies, and you smiled into your phone. You thought you were alone, beautiful and relaxed for once in solitude. I watched, and I watched, and I watched. I memorized your ankles.

O, how we did not understand, then, how we would lose ourselves so quickly, even in all these floating images and films. How could we perceive a life without connectedness? But now we barely remember connection at all. It seems a hazy thing, any picture of us together, any comment I may have left on your page. The robots must have taken them all, I suppose, though I don't remember when. Maybe they made us sad.

Now it's whispered you are somewhere on a sister ship, vice president of something or other. PR? Sales? It doesn't matter. We're not selling anything but time. And I love you still, in a way the beige days can't change. I should have thrown myself off that mountain. I should have known you'd take whatever you could get when it came to power. O Collaborator, O Emmaline. I'd go on, but I have a conference call with Johnson in ten.

Of Stars

I have been so lonely, O gods. I have been like the stars, white-hot with endless longing. Where is my companion? Wishing, now, I could fall to Earth. I spend days with my cheek against the cold plastic laminate of my desk, building a place in my head where a human could actually live. It is a castle, a pink sandstone thing hung with tapestries and fireplaces. It is grand, enormous, warmed by the sun—the Earth's bright sun.

Someone once said—a poet?—that all light is starlight. Does that mean it's all dead on arrival, more echo than embrace? Is light just another way to be alone? I draw the kinds of light in my day planner, crumpling crisp white pages when the light isn't diffuse enough. I use my expensive pens for cross-hatching, trying to spread the light across the cubicles and cafeteria.

Johnson says all this dreaming is hurting my chances of promotion.

Supernova Remains

My father used to hit my mother, hard and often. My mother would counter, strong, with stories for us, stories for herself, knights and champions and magic doorways. They centered, always, around the castle. Or the Castle? They always seemed to be stories about rescue, and all of us were too small to help. When she finally left, rescuing herself at last, my sisters and I kept our ears open for her tales to reach us, sure they were the bread crumbs she'd dropped for us to see the path forward.

When we didn't, we were sure it was we who had failed. And my father too—he who drove her away—he wilted, he shriveled, and he husked without her. It is this the robots cannot understand. That human love is mostly failure. That failure may be very sad, but it is yours, and you hold on to it if you can.

O Emmaline, I know I lost my heart to you, and this is not a metaphor. I know I lost my blood, my bones, my skin cells, my DNA—everything has peeled away from me and stuck to some spectral outline of you, some constellation lost to history long ago. The robots tell us nothing is really lost. All turns, reverses, becomes, dissolves, re-forms, and streams out among the stars. They tell us they have seen it, over and over, the cycle long but eventual. Everything returns in the beginning and the end.

Celestial Coordinates

To be clear, this was never the robots' fault. Not any of it.

Johnson and Bradley said yes to endless cocktails, but only if they came with secretaries. The women liked the way the work stopped them from needing stories and selfies. The men liked the way their wives disappeared into cubes down the hall, liked the way they no longer had to be interesting or thin or emotionally available. People liked the way their children were cared for, and they liked that the robots taught them quickly to learn, and grow, and come to self-sufficiency. The kids weren't sitting in front of screens all damn day, and wasn't that nicer?

The robots didn't understand how small and *analog* human ambition could be, how easy to feed. Of course we dream of filing cabinets and paper trails, the vast most of us. Bigger dreams are hard, are messy with feeling. Connection causes pain.

The robots, I wonder if they ever read Kafka? I don't think there are books here, outside of *What Color Is Your Parachute?* At least, none that I've seen.

Relativity, Special

My mother built herself walls of story and so I will rebuild her story castle, right here in this cubicle. Surely, I can't be the only one dreaming himself out. Surely others will refuse the endless meetings, the swivel chairs, the fluorescent lights, the traffic jams, the built-in ashtrays, the stacks and stacks of paper. Surely someone on this ship wants to feel something more than the smallest feelings. Where, after all, are the humans who built the robots?

Long ago, I decided I would live (many didn't), and that I would live for love. But living so long has begun to cloud that intention. The furniture falls apart in these rooms. The shabbiness shows through. If I don't act soon, the walls will shift and sink, the dreams will dissolve, and I will be left with nothing but stray pixels and this cold hard ship, empty, I suspect, of everyone but me and them.

Emmaline, I am building this castle for us. I plan to scale these walls and escape to you.

Zenith

Space was not prepared to receive us and does not receive us now. To the robots, it is immaterial: we needed to leave the planet, the oceans were swallowing us whole, and so we went. We were given no choice. We are lucky they felt some responsibility for their makers, as clumsy and backward as we are to them.

But for us, who built Elysian Fields for our dead, who tore down our forests and burnt the sky to please the living, who made the robots to make us whole—we might have made another choice. We might have burned along with the world, drowned along with the dead. Are we living now? Landscapes are malleable, organic; a human can make a mark. But we are making nothing.

I shall construct this castle in honor of that memory of earth, the conquest; Earth, the colony. I shall build my walls of red stone and wet sand, of glass and clay and rope and wood—all the things we have thrown away for good. I shall build my walls around that ossuary, the bodies of our saints, our human bones. These relics can be called up at any time. They smell of sky, of grave, of deep wet earth, loamy and brown. I will dig the stars from the sky; I will bury them like seeds and we will grow a new and living home.

Of Stars, Coda

I was ten years old. My grandfather had eyes the color of moons, the result of his blindness. He was a seer, one of those working on the prototypes. He thought we were ready to be relieved. He was happy I would never need to work again. He talked about it, often, the way we would have leisure time at last. I laugh to think of it now, leaving for my Tuesday afternoon brainstorming session.

Sometimes I think we already died, years or eons ago. Sometimes I think we are living on only in dreams, as brains in a jar, or maybe just ones and zeros. I don't like to think past this thought.

Postscript

Emmaline, the HR bot says the person matching your name and description is no longer a person, but a pile of ashes. Emmaline, they won't give me details, won't tell me where and when in time I can ride to rescue you. They tell me lies; they say "old age"; I say Emmaline was young and so am I.

They say, and I swear to you, there is a look of pity in the HR bot's eyes, they say, sir. Sir, we are sorry, but the nineties has been a very long decade.

Mildly Joyful, with Moments of Extraordinary Unhappiness

———————⊷

THE MAN AND WOMAN ARE CHILDLESS AND WEALTHY AND happy. She loves him, and he loves her, in part because of affection, in part because of muscle memory, in part because of their shared personal possessions. They love each other about as much as people who adore things can love other people. She has learned to love things less the older she grows. He has come to depend on them. She is generous and quiet, and he is witty and talkative. They are a good match; all of their friends say so.

They eat out every night at loud restaurants with short menus and long waits. Occasionally, they order in. They live in a nice two-bedroom condo in the city. The master bedroom is full of paintings they've acquired during their travels. Their bed is hand-carved; their sheets are embroidered. The second bedroom is used as a study, and they've filled it with sculpture and books and other beautiful things. They both have high-paying jobs they tolerate, and they travel often, and she plays piano in the evenings while he sings along. It's enough to remind them of their former selves, before they acquired so many things but after they acquired each other.

He is kind to her and she is kind to everybody; if pressed he would say it's the only thing he doesn't like about her. This, he knows, sounds monstrous, but he understands he's borrowed so many better traits from her. He would not use the word jealous, but resentment, yes, perhaps. He only has enough kindness for one person. He supposes that's what love means to him. If he were a good person, he supposes, it would be a trait he would love, this boundless heart. But he isn't a better person. He knows this about himself. She knows this, too, and because she is kind, loves him even more for it.

One day she goes for a walk and she doesn't come back. He assumes she's left, probably with one of the many men she spends her kindness on. Or maybe one of the women. He does not call Missing Persons. He calls her parents and tells them she's run off with a lover. Her parents are horrified; her mother offers to fly into town with a tuna casserole. He will be fine, he assures them; he expected something like this. He has prepared. He hangs up the phone and feels his good bits breaking off, bitterness growing in like brittle new limbs.

Later in the evening, a phone call from the hospital: she's been hit by a car and would he come quickly please to say his goodbyes? He does not dare to come, not now. He does not tell her parents. He hides in his apartment and orders Chinese from their favorite place. The delivery guy inquires after his wife and the man does not answer, instead hands him a ten. Inside his fortune cookie: "What you deserve will find you." He swallows the paper, black ink smeared across the tip of his tongue. His wife dies alone in the early morning.

After the funeral, he buys more things. Anyone would. There is now so much more space to fill. He fills, and fills, with boxes he'll never open, crates he'll never unpack. He buys twenty identical sweaters from Barneys and never picks up the box from the front stoop. The same gray wool cardigan shows up on men and boys throughout the neighborhood that winter.

Eventually, he decides it will be easier to erase her, to undo her. He gives away her things and he tells their friends she was having affairs. He throws away their photo albums. He sells her piano but the movers can't get it out of the window; they shake their heads and depart, sweaty and disappointed. He becomes fixated on the notion of getting the piano gone, any way that he can. He measures it obsessively, plans to chisel wider doorways, break windowpanes. He sketches plans that rival Wile E. Coyote's, all when he's supposed to be working.

Finally, he buys a small ax from the neighborhood hardware store. The young woman working there makes a joke about the frozen sea within us, and he smiles wanly because his wife once bought a throw pillow embroidered with that quote and it had given him some small pleasure then to prove she didn't know where it came from, and that it was a stupid thing to sew onto a pillow. He marches home with purpose, ax very much in hand, and of course no one stops him because he is white and middle-aged and wearing an expensive parka. He proceeds to chop the piano up, no method, just one thunderous chord at a time.

When the police finally force the door, he's sitting in a pile of broken keys and lacquered wood. Someone called about a domestic disturbance, they say, and he shrugs and says, Yes. His wife's ghost hovers just overhead, and she smiles as if in apology, as if to say, *This is all my fault, I deserved it, I asked for it.* But no one is fooled. The room vibrates with something much the opposite of kindness.

The officers flee as the piano keys start to fly, broken bars whirling across the living room. From outside, they see the window darken; the man and his things are obscured by the blizzard of silent notes.

Tour of the Cities We Have Lost

———————————————————

OUR HISTORY IS A HALLWAY. IN THIS VAST SUBTERRANEAN corridor, we keep all the secret places of the world.

This wing, for example, houses our lost cities. The lost city is a thing of power, grown to enormous size through its dislocation from time and people. All the cities we have lost can be found here, all the props and scenery, the backdrops still hiding the concrete walls. The people, though, are long gone. The people's absence is what causes our voices to echo so strangely here. Debussy knew when he wrote *La cathédrale engloutie* how small and dreadful sounds can be, drowned in an empty city without bodies to absorb them.

Here you may visit any city you've ever loved and left. Childhood playthings, cities you built with blocks or bricks or mud or logs, the tiny cities that sprang up around your toy railroad station and its whistling, smoking trains. Cities of discovery, where you first knew love, or suffered loss, or encountered meaning; these are all awaiting you in exactly the condition you found them. Now, of course, if you return to the original and excavate the source, you will find gray skies, pointless architecture, primitive inhabitants, and cumbersome grid structures. But here you will find the sky as blue as it appeared to you the day you met your husband, or your wife, or your lover.

Remembered cities are easy to rebuild. Our true specialty is the difficult cities: cities lost for centuries, cities that existed only in the collective fancies and myths of men. Here we have cities as they were. Here we have cities as we have always imagined them to be. Here, for example, is Camelot: the old, deepening light illuminating silent castle walls, the great table within, where all valor once lived and died. This is a sad place, like any lost city. Here greatness can still be felt seeping out of the soil; here only the trees remember the important things, secrets whispered in the shadow of dawn and shouted through the din of battle. All is still green in Camelot. But only the kind of green that grows over graves, that thrives in the stillness of a finished story.

This way now, a few doors and to your left: this is where we keep Ys. Wicked city once swallowed by the sea; the smell of rot and brine is strong here. The king's daughter, Dahut, once held court in this chamber. The chamber was kept full of bodies writhing in passion and later in pain, but all this flesh has dissolved and only the violent stains spattered across cut marble speak now of

Ys's tragedy. The bronze walls are still whole and polished, the wide gates still flung open, still inviting the floods that swept the city's innards into the ocean. You can feel it. The disease that eats the soul of a city long after the living have vanished.

Come away from there, and follow us to a city that never was. Five doors down and turn the key where it fits inside the doorplate, beneath in the golden knob. Now quickly, look away! At first glance this city will blind you. This is El Dorado, rich in cinnamon and other spices but most of all in gold. The streets, it's true, are paved with it. The luster of this city is both vision and portent. It is the dream of wealth and death that all men dream. It is beautiful, yes, but a bloodless beauty; it has no heart, no heat, no life. A city, yet not a city; it is a prison, a mirage. We keep this one under lock and key, as you can see. A dangerous place, El Dorado. Strong poison in a golden cup.

There are so many secret cities here, once or forever lost. We can take you to Babylon, to Quivira and Cibola, to Shambhala, Thierna Na Oge, and even to Troy as it was. We can show you Xuan Pu, Basilia, Agartha, Shangri-La, Pompeii, and Caritambo, too. Cities consumed by fire and war and water. By avarice and greed and pride. All wiped out, razed, ruined, smashed, shuttered, annihilated and crushed. Gone.

We must carry torches down here, for strong light is a bath these cities can no longer stand. They would crumble to dust in daylight, like old manuscripts and maps. We must wear special gloves to handle the structures of these places, to examine the cafés and sidewalks, the cinema and stadium without risk to their form and integrity. And we must always visit in groups, for these cities can never be seen by one alone. Only for its former crowds will the city slowly stir and come to life, street by street, building by building, like an enormous diorama giving back to us the things we thought we'd lost forever.

Acknowledgments

EVERY BOOK IS AN EXERCISE IN ACCRUING DEBTS YOU CAN'T possibly pay back; instead you write a list of thank-yous and hope in some small way it suffices. Bearing that in mind, thank you to the many editors who worked on, polished, shaped, loved, and published some of these stories: Brian Mihok, Gabriel Blackwell, Roxane Gay, M. Bartley Siegel, Kate Bernheimer, Benjamin Schaefer, Scott Garson, Jeremy John Parker, Tara Laskowski, Lauren Becker, Amanda Miska, Katie Flynn, Morgan Beatty, Aubrey Hirsch, Adam Prince, Richard Thomas, and Josh Pachter. Thank you to my marvelous first readers and longtime trusted friends: Robert Kloss, Erin Fitzgerald, and Steve Himmer. Thank you to Gregory Howard, Lincoln Michel, Joseph Scapelato, Jeff Jackson, Rion Amilcar Scott, Tara Campbell, Sarah Rose Etter, Matt Bell, Kate Zambreno, Penina Roth, Marie-Helene Bertino, and Laura Bogart for reasons varied and numerous.

Thank you to all of the women I know, writers and otherwise; you keep singing in dark times and you keep me sane by doing so. Thank you to the men I know who are fierce allies and feminists: you guys get it. Thank you to all the genderqueer folks I know: this book is very much for you and for everyone tearing down gender norms and barriers.

Thank you to my blurbers, who gave of their time and so generously read this book, no matter how busy they were. Thank you to my fabulous editor, Gina Iaquinta, who worked so hard to make this book a thousand times better. Thank you to the whole team at Liveright; I'm so happy to be working with you all again. Thank you to my agent, Kent Wolf, who will always have the best hair along with the eternal gratitude of all of his writers.

Thank you to my family, especially my mom and dad, who probably still think I'm a morbid weirdo but who have been nothing but supportive of my morbid weirdo pursuits. Thank you to my husband, Christopher, who is the very best human in the world and without whose support and *time* and love I would never, ever have been able to write this book.

And finally, thank you to my daughter, Isadora. This book would not exist without you. I wrote it for you, and for all the daughters, and for all the mothers of daughters, and for all the mothers of mothers of daughters; thank you for carrying the world.